Abandoned

Jules Verne

Abandoned

The present edition is a reproduction of previous publication of this classic work. Minor typographical errors may have been corrected without note; however, for an authentic reading experience the spelling, punctuation, and capitalization have been retained from the original text.

ISBN: 978-1-63637-158-0

INTRODUCTION

The present romance, the second in the Mysterious Island triad, was originally issued in Paris with the title of *L'Abandonné*. Jules Verne's list of stories already ran then to some twenty volumes—a number which has since grown to almost Dumasien proportions. *L'Abandonné*, like its two companion tales, ran its course as a serial through the *Magasin Illustré* of education and recreation, before its issue as a boy's story-book. Its success in both forms seems to have established a record in the race for popularity and a circulation in both the French and English fields of current literature. The present book was translated into English by the late W. H. G. Kingston; and is printed in Everyman's Library by special exclusive arrangement with Messrs. Sampson Low, Marston & Co., Ltd.

1909

CHAPTER I

**Conversation on the Subject of the Bullet—
Construction of a Canoe—Hunting—At the Top of a Kauri—
Nothing to attest the Presence of Man—Neb and Herbert's
Prize—Turning a Turtle—The Turtle disappears—Cyrus
Harding's Explanation.**

It was now exactly seven months since the balloon voyagers
had been thrown on Lincoln Island. During that time,
notwithstanding the researches they had made, no human being
had been discovered. No smoke even had betrayed the presence of
man on the surface of the island. No vestiges of his handiwork
showed that either at an early or at a late period had man lived
there. Not only did it now appear to be uninhabited by any but
themselves, but the colonists were compelled to believe that it never
had been inhabited. And now, all this scaffolding of reasonings fell
before a simple ball of metal, found in the body of an inoffensive
rodent! In fact, this bullet must have issued from a firearm, and who
but a human being could have used such a weapon?

When Pencroft had placed the bullet on the table, his
companions looked at it with intense astonishment. All the
consequences likely to result from this incident, notwithstanding its
apparent insignificance, immediately took possession of their
minds. The sudden apparition of a supernatural being could not
have startled them more completely.

Cyrus Harding did not hesitate to give utterance to the
suggestions which this fact, at once surprising and unexpected,
could not fail to raise in his mind. He took the bullet, turned it over
and over, rolled it between his finger and thumb; then, turning to
Pencroft, he asked,—

"Are you sure that the peccary wounded by this bullet was not
more than three months old?"

"Not more, captain," replied Pencroft. "It was still sucking its
mother when I found it in the trap."

"Well," said the engineer, "that proves that within three
months a gun-shot was fired in Lincoln Island."

"And that a bullet," added Gideon Spilett, "wounded, though
not mortally, this little animal."

"That is unquestionable," said Cyrus Harding, "and these are
the deductions which must be drawn from this incident: that the
island was inhabited before our arrival, or that men have landed

1

here within three months. Did these men arrive here voluntarily or involuntarily, by disembarking on the shore or by being wrecked? This point can only be cleared up later. As to what they were, Europeans or Malays, enemies or friends of our race, we cannot possibly guess; and if they still inhabit the island, or if they have left it, we know not. But these questions are of too much importance to be allowed to remain long unsettled."

"No! a hundred times no! a thousand times no!" cried the sailor, springing up from the table. "There are no other men than ourselves on Lincoln Island! By my faith! The island isn't large, and if it had been inhabited, we should have seen some of the inhabitants long before this!"

"In fact, the contrary would be very astonishing," said Herbert.

"But it would be much more astonishing, I should think," observed the reporter, "that this peccary should have been born with a bullet in its inside!"

"At least," said Neb seriously, "if Pencroft has not had—"

"Look here, Neb," burst out Pencroft. "Do you think I could have a bullet in my jaw for five or six months without finding it out? Where could it be hidden?" he asked opening his mouth to show the two-and-thirty teeth with which it was furnished. "Look well, Neb, and if you find one hollow tooth in this set, I will let you pull out half a dozen!"

"Neb's supposition is certainly inadmissible," replied Harding, who, notwithstanding the gravity of his thoughts, could not restrain a smile. "It is certain that a gun has been fired in the island, within three months at most. But I am inclined to think that the people who landed on this coast were only here a very short time ago, or that they just touched here; for if, when we surveyed the island from the summit of Mount Franklin, it had been inhabited, we should have seen them or we should have been seen ourselves. It is therefore probable that within only a few weeks castaways have been thrown by a storm on some part of the coast. However that may be, it is of consequence to us to have this point settled."

"I think that we should act with caution," said the reporter.

"Such is my advice," replied Cyrus Harding, "for it is to be feared that Malay pirates have landed on the island!"

"Captain," asked the sailor, "would it not be a good plan, before setting out, to build a canoe in which we could either ascend the river, or, if we liked, coast round the island? It will not do to be unprovided."

"Your idea is good, Pencroft," replied the engineer, "but

we cannot wait for that. It would take at least a month to build a boat."

"Yes, a real boat," replied the sailor; "but we do not want one for a sea voyage, and in five days at the most, I will undertake to construct a canoe fit to navigate the Mercy."

"Five days," cried Neb, "to build a boat?"

"Yes, Neb; a boat in the Indian fashion."

"Of wood?" asked the negro, looking still unconvinced.

"Of wood," replied Pencroft, "or rather of bark. I repeat, captain, that in five days the work will be finished!"

"In five days, then, be it," replied the engineer.

"But till that time we must be very watchful," said Herbert.

"Very watchful indeed, my friends," replied Harding; "and I beg you to confine your hunting excursions to the neighbourhood of Granite House."

The dinner ended less gaily than Pencroft had hoped.

So, then, the island was, or had been, inhabited by others than the settlers. Proved as it was by the incident of the bullet, it was hereafter an unquestionable fact, and such a discovery could not but cause great uneasiness amongst the colonists.

Cyrus Harding and Gideon Spilett, before sleeping, conversed long about the matter. They asked themselves if by chance this incident might not have some connection with the inexplicable way in which the engineer had been saved, and the other peculiar circumstances which had struck them at different times. However Cyrus Harding, after having discussed the pros and cons of the question, ended by saying,—

"In short, would you like to know my opinion, my dear Spilett?"

"Yes, Cyrus."

"Well, then, it is this: however minutely we explore the island, we shall find nothing."

The next day Pencroft set to work. He did not mean to build a boat with boards and planking, but simply a flat-bottomed canoe, which would be well suited for navigating the Mercy—above all, for approaching its source, where the water would naturally be shallow. Pieces of bark, fastened one to the other, would form a light boat; and in case of natural obstacles, which would render a portage necessary, it would be easily carried. Pencroft intended to secure the pieces of bark by means of nails, to insure the canoe being water-tight.

It was first necessary to select the trees which would afford a strong and supple bark for the work. Now the last storm had

3

brought down a number of large birch trees, the bark of which would be perfectly suited for their purpose. Some of these trees lay on the ground, and they had only to be barked, which was the most difficult thing of all, owing to the imperfect tools which the settlers possessed. However, they overcame all difficulties.

Whilst the sailor, seconded by the engineer, thus occupied himself without losing an hour, Gideon Spilett and Herbert were not idle. They were made purveyors to the colony. The reporter could not but admire the boy, who had acquired great skill in handling the bow and spear. Herbert also showed great courage and much of that presence of mind which may justly be called "the reasoning of bravery." These two companions of the chase, remembering Cyrus Harding's recommendations, did not go beyond a radius of two miles round Granite House; but the borders of the forest furnished a sufficient tribute of agouties, capybaras, kangaroos, peccaries, etc.; and if the result from the traps was less than during the cold, still the warren yielded its accustomed quota, which might have fed all the colony in Lincoln Island.

Often during these excursions, Herbert talked with Gideon Spilett on the incident of the bullet, and the deductions which the engineer drew from it, and one day—it was the 26th of October—he said,—

"But, Mr. Spilett, do you not think it very extraordinary that, if any castaways have landed on the island, they have not yet shown themselves near Granite House?"

"Very astonishing if they are still here," replied the reporter, "but not astonishing at all if they are here no longer!"

"So you think that these people have already quitted the island?" returned Herbert.

"It is more than probable, my boy; for if their stay was prolonged, and above all, if they were still here, some accident would have at last betrayed their presence."

"But if they were able to go away," observed the lad, "they could not have been castaways."

"No, Herbert; or, at least, they were what might be called provisional castaways. It is very possible that a storm may have driven them to the island without destroying their vessel, and that, the storm over, they went away again."

"I must acknowledge one thing," said Herbert, "it is that Captain Harding appears rather to fear than desire the presence of human beings on our island."

"In short," responded the reporter, "there are only Malays

who frequent these seas, and those fellows are ruffians which it is best to avoid."

"It is not impossible, Mr. Spilett," said Herbert, "that some day or other we may find traces of their landing."

"I do not say no, my boy. A deserted camp, the ashes of a fire, would put us on the track, and this is what we will look for in our next expedition."

The day on which the hunters spoke thus, they were in a part of the forest near the Mercy, remarkable for its beautiful trees. There, among others, rose, to a height of nearly 200 feet above the ground, some of those superb coniferæ, to which, in New Zealand, the natives give the name of Kauris.

"I have an idea, Mr. Spilett," said Herbert. "If I were to climb to the top of one of these kauris, I could survey the country for an immense distance round."

"The idea is good," replied the reporter; "but could you climb to the top of those giants?"

"I can at least try," replied Herbert.

The light and active boy then sprang on the first branches, the arrangement of which made the ascent of the kauri easy, and in a few minutes he arrived at the summit, which emerged from the immense plain of verdure.

From this elevated situation his gaze extended over all the southern portion of the island, from Claw Cape on the south-east, to Reptile End on the south-west. To the north-west rose Mount Franklin, which concealed a great part of the horizon.

But Herbert, from the height of his observatory, could examine all the yet unknown portion of the island which might have given shelter to the strangers whose presence they suspected.

The lad looked attentively. There was nothing in sight on the sea, not a sail, neither on the horizon nor near the island. However, as the bank of trees hid the shore, it was possible that a vessel, especially if deprived of her masts, might lie close to the land and thus be invisible to Herbert.

Neither in the forests of the Far West was anything to be seen. The wood formed an impenetrable screen, measuring several square miles, without a break or an opening. It was impossible even to follow the course of the Mercy, or to ascertain in what part of the mountain it took its source. Perhaps other creeks also ran towards the west, but they could not be seen.

But at last, if all indication of an encampment escaped Herbert's sight, could he not even catch a glimpse of smoke, the faintest trace of which would be easily discernible in the pure atmosphere?

For an instant Herbert thought he could perceive a slight smoke in the west, but a more attentive examination showed that he was mistaken. He strained his eyes in every direction, and his sight was excellent. No, decidedly there was nothing there.

Herbert descended to the foot of the kauri, and the two sportsmen returned to Granite House. There Cyrus Harding listened to the lad's account, shook his head and said nothing. It was very evident that no decided opinion could be pronounced on this question until after a complete exploration of the island.

Two days after—the 28th of October—another incident occurred, for which an explanation was again required.

Whilst strolling along the shore about two miles from Granite House, Herbert and Neb were fortunate enough to capture a magnificent specimen of the order of chelonia. It was a turtle of the species Midas, the edible green turtle, so called from the colour both of its shell and fat.

Herbert caught sight of this turtle as it was crawling among the rocks to reach the sea.

"Help, Neb, help!" he cried.

Neb ran up.

"What a fine animal!" said Neb; "but how are we to catch it?"

"Nothing is easier, Neb," replied Herbert. "We have only to turn the turtle on its back, and it cannot possibly get away. Take your spear and do as I do."

The reptile, aware of danger, had retired between its carapace and plastron. They no longer saw its head or feet, and it was motionless as a rock.

Herbert and Neb then drove their sticks underneath the animal, and by their united efforts managed without difficulty to turn it on its back. The turtle, which was three feet in length, would have weighed at least four hundred pounds.

"Capital!" cried Neb; "this is something which will rejoice friend Pencroft's heart."

In fact, the heart of friend Pencroft could not fail to be rejoiced, for the flesh of the turtle, which feeds on wrack-grass, is extremely savoury. At this moment the creature's head could be seen, which was small, flat, but widened behind by the large temporal fossæ hidden under the long roof.

"And now, what shall we do with our prize?" said Neb. "We can't drag it to Granite House!"

"Leave it here, since it cannot turn over," replied Herbert, "and we will come back with the cart to fetch it."

"That is the best plan."

However, for greater precaution, Herbert took the trouble, which Neb deemed superfluous, to wedge up the animal with great stones, after which the two hunters returned to Granite House, following the beach, which the tide had left uncovered. Herbert, wishing to surprise Pencroft, said nothing about the "superb specimen of a chelonian" which they had turned over on the sand, but, two hours later, he and Neb returned with the cart to the place where they had left it. The "superb specimen of a chelonian" was no longer there!

Neb and Herbert stared at each other first, then they stared about them. It was just at this spot that the turtle had been left. The lad even found the stones which he had used, and therefore he was certain of not being mistaken.

"Well!" said Neb, "these beasts can turn themselves over, then?"

"It appears so," replied Herbert, who could not understand it at all, and was gazing at the stones scattered on the sand.

"Well, Pencroft will be disgusted!"

"And Captain Harding will perhaps be very perplexed how to explain this disappearance" thought Herbert.

"Look here," said Neb, who wished to hide his ill-luck, "we won't speak about it."

"On the contrary, Neb we must speak about it," replied Herbert.

And the two, taking the cart, which there was now no use for, returned to Granite House.

Arrived at the dockyard, where the engineer and the sailor were working together Herbert recounted what had happened.

"Oh! the stupids!" cried the sailor, "to have let at least fifty meals escape!"

"But, Pencroft," replied Neb, "it wasn't our fault that the beast got away, as I tell you, we had turned it over on its back!"

"Then you didn't turn it over enough!" returned the obstinate sailor.

"Not enough!" cried Herbert.

And he told how he had taken care to wedge up the turtle with stones.

"It is a miracle, then!" replied Pencroft.

"I thought, captain," said Herbert, "that turtles, once placed

7

on their backs, could not regain their feet, especially when they are of a large size?"

"That is true, my boy," replied Cyrus Harding.

"Then how did it manage?"

"At what distance from the sea did you leave this turtle?" asked the engineer, who, having suspended his work, was reflecting on this incident.

"Fifteen feet at the most," replied Herbert.

"And the tide was low at the time?"

"Yes, captain."

"Well," replied the engineer, "what the turtle could not do on the sand it might have been able to do in the water. It turned over when the tide overtook it, and then quietly returned to the deep sea."

"Oh! what stupids we were!" cried Neb.

"That is precisely what I had the honour of telling you before!" returned the sailor.

Cyrus Harding had given this explanation, which, no doubt, was admissible. But was he himself convinced of the accuracy of this explanation? It cannot be said that he was.

CHAPTER II

First Trial of the Canoe—A Wreck on the Coast—Towing—Flotsam Point—Inventory of the Case: Tools, Weapons, Instruments, Clothes, Books, Utensils—What Pencroft misses—The Gospel—A Verse from the Sacred Book.

On the 9th of October the bark canoe was entirely finished. Pencroft had kept his promise, and a light boat, the shell of which was joined together by the flexible twigs of the crejimba, had been constructed in five days. A seat in the stern, a second seat in the middle to preserve the equilibrium, a third seat in the bows, rowlocks for the two oars, a scull to steer with, completed the little craft, which was twelve feet long, and did not weigh more than 200 pounds.

The operation of launching it was extremely simple. The canoe was carried to the beach and laid on the sand before Granite House, and the rising tide floated it. Pencroft, who leapt in directly, manœuvred it with the scull and declared it to be just the thing for the purpose to which they wished to put it.

"Hurrah!" cried the sailor, who did not disdain to celebrate thus his own triumph. "With this we could go round—"

"The world?" asked Gideon Spilett.

"No, the island. Some stones for ballast, a mast, and a sail, which the captain will make for us some day, and we shall go splendidly! Well, captain—and you, Mr. Spilett; and you, Herbert; and you, Neb—aren't you coming to try our new vessel? Come along! we must see if it will carry all five of us!"

This was certainly a trial which ought to be made. Pencroft soon brought the canoe to the shore by a narrow passage among the rocks, and it was agreed that they should make a trial of the boat that day by following the shore as far as the first point at which the rocks of the south ended.

As they embarked, Neb cried,—

"But your boat leaks rather, Pencroft."

"That's nothing, Neb," replied the sailor; "the wood will get seasoned. In two days there won't be a single leak, and our boat will have no more water in her than there is in the stomach of a drunkard. Jump in!"

They were soon all seated, and Pencroft shoved off. The weather was magnificent, the sea as calm as if its waters were

9

contained within the narrow limits of a lake. Thus the boat could proceed with as much security as if it was ascending the tranquil current of the Mercy.

Neb took one of the oars, Herbert the other, and Pencroft remained in the stern in order to use the skull.

The sailor first crossed the channel, and steered close to the southern point of the islet. A light breeze blew from the south. No roughness was found either in the channel or the green sea. A long swell, which the canoe scarcely felt, as it was heavily laden, rolled regularly over the surface of the water. They pulled out about half a mile distant from the shore, that they might have a good view of Mount Franklin.

Pencroft afterwards returned towards the mouth of the river. The boat then skirted the shore, which, extending to the extreme point, hid all Tadorn's Fens.

This point, of which the distance was increased by the irregularity of the coast, was nearly three miles from the Mercy. The settlers resolved to go to its extremity, and only go beyond it as much as was necessary to take a rapid survey of the coast as far as Claw Cape.

The canoe followed the windings of the shore, avoiding the rocks which fringed it, and which the rising tide began to cover. The cliff gradually sloped away from the mouth of the river to the point. This was formed of granite rocks, capriciously distributed, very different from the cliff at Prospect Heights, and of an extremely wild aspect. It might have been said that an immense cartload of rocks had been emptied out there. There was no vegetation on this sharp promontory, which projected two miles from the forest, and it thus represented a giant's arm stretched out from a leafy sleeve.

The canoe, impelled by the two oars, advanced without difficulty. Gideon Spilett, pencil in one hand and note-book in the other, sketched the coast in bold strokes. Neb, Herbert, and Pencroft chatted, whilst examining this part of their domain, which was new to them, and, in proportion as the canoe proceeded towards the south, the two Mandible Capes appeared to move, and surround Union Bay more closely.

As to Cyrus Harding, he did not speak; he simply gazed, and by the mistrust which his look expressed, it appeared that he was examining some strange country.

In the meanwhile, after a voyage of three quarters of an hour, the canoe reached the extremity of the point, and Pencroft was preparing to return, when Herbert, rising, pointed to a black object, saying,—

"What do I see down there on the beach?"

All eyes turned towards the point indicated.

"Why," said the reporter, "there is something. It looks like part of a wreck half buried in the sand."

"Ah!" cried Pencroft, "I see what it is!"

"What?" asked Neb.

"Barrels, barrels, which perhaps are full," replied the sailor.

"Pull to the shore, Pencroft!" said Cyrus.

A few strokes of the oar brought the canoe into a little creek, and its passengers leapt on shore.

Pencroft was not mistaken. Two barrels were there, half buried in the sand, but still firmly attached to a large chest, which, sustained by them, had floated to the moment when it stranded on the beach.

"There has been a wreck, then, in some part of the island," said Herbert.

"Evidently," replied Spilett.

"But what's in this chest?" cried Pencroft, with very natural impatience. "What's in this chest? It is shut up, and nothing to open it with! Well, perhaps a stone—"

And the sailor, raising a heavy block, was about to break in one of the sides of the chest, when the engineer arrested his hand.

"Pencroft," said he, "can you restrain your impatience for one hour only?"

"But, captain, just think! Perhaps there is everything we want in there!"

"We shall find that out, Pencroft," replied the engineer; "but trust to me, and do not break the chest, which may be useful to us. We must convey it to Granite House, where we can open it easily and without breaking it. It is quite prepared for a voyage, and, since it has floated here, it may just as well float to the mouth of the river."

"You are right, captain, and I was wrong, as usual," replied the sailor.

The engineer's advice was good. In fact, the canoe probably would not have been able to contain the articles possibly enclosed in the chest, which doubtless was heavy, since two empty barrels were required to buoy it up. It was, therefore, much better to tow it to the beach at Granite House.

And now, whence had this chest come? That was the important question Cyrus Harding and his companions looked attentively around them, and examined the shore for several hundred steps. No other articles or pieces of wreck could be found.

Herbert and Neb climbed a high rock to survey the sea, but there was nothing in sight—neither a dismasted vessel nor a ship under sail.

However, there was no doubt that there had been a wreck Perhaps this incident was connected with that of the bullet? Perhaps strangers had landed on another part of the island? Perhaps they were still there? But the thought which came naturally to the settlers was, that these strangers could not be Malay pirates, for the chest was evidently of American or European make.

All the party returned to the chest, which was of an unusually large size. It was made of oak wood, very carefully closed and covered with a thick hide, which was secured by copper nails. The two great barrels, hermetically sealed, but which sounded hollow and empty, were fastened to its sides by strong ropes knotted with a skill which Pencroft directly pronounced sailors alone could exhibit. It appeared to be in a perfect state of preservation, which was explained by the fact that it had stranded on a sandy beach, and not among rocks. They had no doubt whatever, on examining it carefully, that it had not been long in the water, and that its arrival on this coast was recent. The water did not appear to have penetrated to the inside, and the articles which it contained were no doubt uninjured.

It was evident that this chest had been thrown overboard from some dismasted vessel driven towards the island, and that, in the hope that it would reach the land, where they might afterwards find it, the passengers had taken the precaution to buoy it up by means of this floating apparatus.

"We will tow this chest to Granite House," said the engineer, "where we can make an inventory of its contents, then, if we discover any of the survivors from the supposed wreck, we can return it to those to whom it belongs. If we find no one—"

"We will keep it for ourselves!" cried Pencroft "But what in the world can there be in it?"

The sea was already approaching the chest, and the high tide would evidently float it. One of the ropes which fastened the barrels was partly unlashed and used as a cable to unite the floating apparatus with the canoe. Pencroft and Neb then dug away the sand with their oars, so as to facilitate the moving of the chest, towing which the boat soon began to double the point to which the name of Flotsam Point was given.

The chest was heavy, and the barrels were scarcely sufficient to keep it above water. The sailor also feared every instant that it would get loose and sink to the bottom of the sea. But happily his fears were not realised, and an hour and a half after they set out—all that time had been taken up in going a distance of three miles—the boat touched the beach below Granite House.

Canoe and chest were then hauled up on the sand, and as the tide was then going out, they were soon left high and dry. Neb, hurrying home, brought back some tools with which to open the chest in such a way that it might be injured as little as possible, and they proceeded to its inventory. Pencroft did not try to hide that he was greatly excited.

The sailor began by detaching the two barrels, which, being in good condition, would of course be of use. Then the locks were forced with a cold chisel and hammer, and the lid thrown back. A second casing of zinc lined the interior of the chest, which had been evidently arranged that the articles which it enclosed might under any circumstances be sheltered from damp.

"Oh!" cried Neb, "suppose it's jam!".

"I hope not," replied the reporter.

"If only there was—" said the sailor in a low voice.

"What?" asked Neb, who overheard him.

"Nothing!"

The covering of zinc was torn off and thrown back over the sides of the chest, and by degrees numerous articles of very varied character were produced and strewn about on the sand. At each new object Pencroft uttered fresh hurrahs, Herbert clapped his hands, and Neb danced—like a nigger. There were books which made Herbert wild with joy, and cooking utensils which Neb covered with kisses!

In short, the colonists had reason to be extremely satisfied, for this chest contained tools, weapons, instruments, clothes, books; and this is the exact list of them as stated in Gideon Spilett's note-book:—

Tools:—

knives with several blades, 2 woodmen's axes, 2 carpenter's hatchets, 3 planes, 2 adzes, 1 twibil or mattock, 6 chisels, 2 files, 3 hammers, 3 gimlets, 2 augers, 10 bags of nails and screws, 3 saws of different sizes, 2 boxes of needles.

Weapons:—2 flint-lock guns, 2 for percussion caps, 2 breech-loader carbines, boarding cutlasses, 4 sabres, 2 barrels of powder, each containing twenty-five pounds; 12 boxes of percussion caps.

Instruments:—1 sextant, 1 double opera-glass, 1 telescope, 1 box of mathematical instruments, 1 mariner's compass, 1 Fahrenheit thermometer, 1 aneroid barometer, 1 box containing a photographic apparatus, object-glass, plates, chemicals, etc.

13

Clothes:—2 dozen shirts of a peculiar material resembling wool, but evidently of a vegetable origin; 3 dozen stockings of the same material.

Utensils:—1 iron pot, 6 copper saucepans, 3 iron dishes, 10 metal plates, 2 kettles, 1 portable stove, 6 table-knives.

Books:—1 Bible, 1 atlas, 1 dictionary of the different Polynesian idioms, 1 dictionary of natural science, in six volumes; 3 reams of white paper, 2 books with blank pages.

"It must be allowed," said the reporter, after the inventory had been made, "that the owner of this chest was a practical man! Tools, weapons, instruments, clothes, utensils, books—nothing is wanting! It might really be said that he expected to be wrecked, and had prepared for it beforehand."

"Nothing is wanting, indeed," murmured Cyrus Harding thoughtfully.

"And for a certainty," added Herbert, "the vessel which carried this chest and its owner was not a Malay pirate!"

"Unless," said Pencroft, "the owner had been taken prisoner by pirates—"

"That is not admissible," replied the reporter. "It is more probable that an American or European vessel has been driven into this quarter, and that her passengers, wishing to save necessaries at least, prepared this chest and threw it overboard."

"Is that your opinion, captain?" asked Herbert.

"Yes, my boy," replied the engineer, "that may have been the case. It is possible that at the moment, or in expectation of a wreck, they collected into this chest different articles of the greatest use in hopes of finding it again on the coast—"

"Even the photographic box!" exclaimed the sailor incredulously.

"As to that apparatus," replied Harding, "I do not quite see the use of it; and a more complete supply of clothes or more abundant ammunition would have been more valuable to us as well as to any other castaways!"

"But isn't there any mark or direction on these instruments, tools, or books, which would tell us something about them?" asked Gideon Spilett.

That might be ascertained. Each article was carefully examined, especially the books, instruments and weapons. Neither the weapons nor the instruments, contrary to the usual custom, bore the name of the maker; they were, besides, in a perfect state, and did not appear to have been used. The same peculiarity marked the tools and utensils; all were new, which proved that the articles had not been taken by chance and thrown into the chest, but, on the contrary, that the choice of the things had been well considered and arranged with care. This was also indicated by a second case of metal which had preserved them from damp, and which could not have been soldered in a moment of haste.

As to the dictionaries of natural science and Polynesian idioms, both were English, but they neither bore the name of the publisher nor the date of publication.

The same with the Bible printed in English, in quarto, remarkable in a typographical point of view, and which appeared to have been often used.

The atlas was a magnificent work, comprising maps of every country in the world, and several planispheres arranged upon Mercator's projection, aid of which the nomenclature was in French—but which also bore neither date nor name of publisher.

There was nothing, therefore, on these different articles by which they could be traced and nothing consequently of a nature to show the nationality of the vessel which must have recently passed these shores.

But, wherever the chest might have come from, it was a treasure to the settlers on Lincoln Island. Till then, by making use of the productions of nature, they had created everything for themselves, and, thanks to their intelligence, they had managed without difficulty. But did it not appear as if Providence had wished to reward them by sending them these productions of human industry? Their thanks rose unanimously to Heaven.

However, one of them was not quite satisfied: it was Pencroft. It appeared that the chest did not contain some thing which he evidently held in great esteem, for in proportion as they approached the bottom of the box, his hurrahs diminished in heartiness, and, the inventory finished, he was heard to mutter these words—

"That's all very fine, but you can see that there is nothing for me in that box!"

This led Neb to say,—

"Why, friend Pencroft, what more do you expect?"

"Half a pound of tobacco," replied Pencroft seriously, "and nothing would have been wanting to complete my happiness."

No one could help laughing at this speech of the sailor's.

But the result of this discovery of the chest was, that it was more than ever necessary to explore the island thoroughly. It was therefore agreed that the next morning at break of day they should set out, by ascending the Mercy so as to reach the western shore. If any castaways had landed on the coast, it was to be feared they were without resources, and it was therefore the more necessary to carry help to them without delay.

During the day the different articles were carried to Granite House, where they were methodically arranged in the great hall.

This day—the 29th of October—happened to be a Sunday, and, before going to bed, Herbert asked the engineer if he would not read them something from the Gospel.

"Willingly," replied Cyrus Harding.

He took the sacred volume, and was about to open it, when Pencroft stopped him, saying,—

"Captain, I am superstitious. Open at random and read the first verse which your eye falls upon. We will see if it applies to our situation."

Cyrus Harding smiled at the sailor's idea, and, yielding to his wish, he opened exactly at a place where the leaves were separated by a marker.

Immediately his eyes were attracted by a cross which, made with a pencil, was placed against the eighth verse of the seventh chapter of the Gospel of St. Matthew. He read the verse, which was this:—

"For every one that asketh receiveth; and he that seeketh findeth."

CHAPTER III

The Start—The rising Tide—Elms and different Plants—The Jacamar—Aspect of the Forest—Gigantic Eucalypti—The Reason they are called "Fever Trees"—Troops of Monkeys—A Waterfall—The Night Encampment.

The next day, the 30th of October, all was ready for the proposed exploring expedition, which recent events had rendered so necessary. In fact, things had so come about that the settlers in Lincoln Island no longer needed help for themselves, but were even able to carry it to others.

It was therefore agreed that they should ascend the Mercy as far as the river was navigable. A great part of the distance would thus be traversed without fatigue, and the explorers could transport their provisions and arms to an advanced point in the west of the island.

It was necessary to think not only of the things which they should take with them, but also of those which they might have by chance to bring back to Granite House. If there had been a wreck on the coast, as was supposed, there would be many things cast up, which would be lawfully their prizes. In the event of this, the cart would have been of more use than the light canoe, but it was heavy and clumsy to drag, and therefore more difficult to use; this led Pencroft to express his regret that the chest had not contained, besides "his half-pound of tobacco," a pair of strong New Jersey horses, which would have been very useful to the colony!

The provisions, which Neb had already packed up, consisted of a store of meat and of several gallons of beer, that is to say, enough to sustain them for three days, the time which Harding assigned for the expedition. They hoped besides to supply themselves on the road, and Neb took care not to forget the portable stove.

The only tools the settlers took were the two woodmen's axes, which they could use to cut a path through the thick forests, as also the instruments, the telescope and pocket-compass.

For weapons they selected the two flint-lock guns, which were likely to be more useful to them than the percussion fowling-pieces, the first only requiring flints which could be easily replaced, and the latter needing fulminating caps, a frequent use of which would soon exhaust their limited stock. However, they took also one of the carbines and some cartridges. As to the powder, of which there was about fifty pounds in the barrel, a small supply of it had to be taken, but the engineer hoped to manufacture an explosive substance which would allow them to husband it. To the firearms were added the five cutlasses well sheathed in leather, and, thus supplied, the settlers could venture into the vast forest with some chance of success.

It is useless to add that Pencroft, Herbert, and Neb, thus armed, were at the summit of their happiness, although Cyrus Harding made them promise not to fire a shot unless it was necessary.

At six in the morning the canoe put off from the shore; all had embarked, including Top, and they proceeded to the mouth of the Mercy.

The tide had begun to come up half an hour before. For several hours, therefore, there would be a current, which it was well to profit by, for later the ebb would make it difficult to ascend the river. The tide was already strong, for in three days the moon would be full, and it was enough to keep the boat in the centre of the current, where it floated swiftly along between the high banks without its being necessary to increase its speed by the aid of the oars. In a few minutes the explorers arrived at the angle formed by the Mercy, and exactly at the place where, seven months before, Pencroft had made his first raft of wood.

After this sudden angle the river widened and flowed under the shade of great evergreen firs.

The aspect of the banks was magnificent. Cyrus Harding and his companions could not but admire the lovely effects so easily produced by nature with water and trees. As they advanced the forest element diminished. On the right bank of the river grew magnificent specimens of the ulmaceæ tribe, the precious elm, so valuable to builders, and which withstands well the action of water. Then there were numerous groups belonging to the same family, amongst others one in particular, the fruit of which produces a very useful oil. Further on, Herbert remarked the lardizabala, a twining shrub which, when bruised in water, furnishes excellent cordage; and two or three ebony trees of a beautiful black, crossed with capricious veins.

From time to time, in certain places where the landing was easy, the canoe was stopped, when Gideon Spilett, Herbert, and Pencroft, their guns in their hands, and preceded by Top, jumped on shore. Without expecting game, some useful plant might be met with, and the young naturalist was delighted with discovering a sort of wild spinage, belonging to the order of chenopodiaceæ, and numerous specimens of cruciferæ, belonging to the cabbage tribe, which it would certainly be possible to cultivate by transplanting. There were cresses, horse-radish, turnips, and lastly, little branching hairy stalks, scarcely more than three feet high, which produced brownish grains.

"Do you know what this plant is?" asked Herbert of the sailor.

"Tobacco!" cried Pencroft, who evidently had never seen his favourite plant except in the bowl of his pipe.

"No, Pencroft," replied Herbert; "this is not tobacco, it is mustard."

"Mustard be hanged!" returned the sailor; "but if by chance you happen to come across a tobacco-plant, my boy, pray don't scorn that!"

"We shall find it some day!" said Gideon Spilett.

"Well!" exclaimed Pencroft, "when that day comes, I do not know what more will be wanting in our island!"

These different plants, which had been carefully rooted, up, were carried to the canoe, where Cyrus Harding had remained buried in thought.

The reporter, Herbert, and Pencroft in this manner frequently disembarked, sometimes on the right bank, sometimes on the left bank of the Mercy.

The latter was less abrupt, but the former more wooded. The engineer ascertained by consulting his pocket compass that the direction of the river from the first turn was obviously south-west and north-east, and nearly straight for a length of about three miles. But it was to be supposed that this direction changed beyond that point, and that the Mercy continued to the north-west, towards the spurs of Mount Franklin, among which the river rose.

During one of these excursions, Gideon Spilett managed to get hold of two couples of living gallinaceæ. They were birds with long, thin beaks, lengthened necks, short wings, and without any appearance of a tail. Herbert rightly gave them the name of tinamons, and it was resolved that they should be the first tenants of their future poultry yard.

But till then the guns had not spoken, and the first report which awoke the echoes of the forest of the Far West was provoked by the appearance of a beautiful bird, resembling the kingfisher.

"I recognise him!" cried Pencroft, and it seemed as if his gun went off by itself.

"What do you recognise?" asked the reporter.

"The bird which escaped us on our first excursion, and from which we gave the name to that part of the forest."

"A jacamar!" cried Herbert.

19

It was indeed a jacamar, of which the plumage shines with a metallic lustre. A shot brought it to the ground, and Top carried it to the canoe. At the same time half a dozen lories were brought down. The lory is of the size of a pigeon, the plumage dashed with green, part of the wings crimson, and its crest bordered with white. To the young boy belonged the honour of this shot, and he was proud enough of it. Lories are better food than the jacamar, the flesh of which is rather tough, but it was difficult to persuade Pencroft that he had not killed the king of eatable birds. It was ten o'clock in the morning when the canoe reached a second angle of the Mercy, nearly five miles from its mouth. Here a halt was made for breakfast under the shade of some splendid trees. The river still measured from sixty to seventy feet in breadth, and its bed from five to six feet in depth. The engineer had observed that it was increased by numerous affluents, but they were unnavigable, being simply little streams. As to the forest, including Jacamar Wood, as well as the forests of the Far West, it extended as far as the eye could reach. In no place, either in the depths of the forest or under the trees on the banks of the Mercy, was the presence of man revealed. The explorers could not discover one suspicious trace. It was evident that the woodman's axe had never touched these trees, that the pioneer's knife had never severed the creepers hanging from one trunk to another in the midst of tangled brushwood and long grass. If castaways had landed on the island, they could not have yet quitted the shore and it was not in the woods that the survivors of the supposed shipwreck should be sought.

The engineer therefore manifested some impatience to reach the western coast of Lincoln Island, which was at least five miles distant according to his estimation.

The voyage was continued, and as the Mercy appeared to flow not towards the shore, but rather towards Mount Franklin, it was decided that they should use the boat as long as there was enough water under its keel to float it. It was both fatigue spared and time gained, for they would have been obliged to cut a path through the thick wood with their axes. But soon the flow completely failed them either the tide was going down, and it was about the hour, or it could no longer be felt at this distance from the mouth of the Mercy. They had therefore to make use of the oars, Herbert and Neb each took one, and Pencroft took the scull. The forest soon became less dense, the trees grew further apart and often quite isolated. But the further they were from each other the more magnificent they appeared, profiting, as they did, by the free, pure air which circulated around them.

What splendid specimens of the Flora of this latitude! Certainly their presence would have been enough for a botanist to name without hesitation the parallel which traversed Lincoln Island.

"Eucalypti!" cried Herbert.

They were, in fact, those splendid trees, the giants of the extra-tropical zone, the congeners of the Australian and New Zealand eucalyptus, both situated under the same latitude as Lincoln Island. Some rose to a height of two hundred feet. Their trunks at the base measured twenty feet in circumference, and their bark was covered by a network of furrows containing a red, sweet-smelling gum. Nothing is more wonderful or more singular than those enormous specimens of the order of the myrtaceæ, with their leaves placed vertically and not horizontally, so that an edge and not a surface looks upwards, the effect being that the sun's rays penetrate more freely among the trees.

The ground at the foot of the eucalypti was carpeted with grass, and from the bushes escaped flights of little birds, which glittered in the sunlight like winged rubies.

"These are something like trees!" cried Neb; "but are they good for anything?"

"Pooh!" replied Pencroft. "Of course there are vegetable giants as well as human giants, and they are no good, except to show themselves at fairs!"

"I think that you are mistaken, Pencroft," replied Gideon Spilett, "and that the wood of the eucalyptus has begun to be very advantageously employed in cabinet-making."

"And I may add," said Herbert, "that the eucalyptus belongs to a family which comprises many useful members; the guava-tree, from whose fruit guava jelly is made; the clove-tree, which produces the spice; the pomegranate-tree, which bears pomegranates; the Eugeacia Cauliflora, the fruit of which is used in making a tolerable wine; the Ugui myrtle, which contains an excellent alcoholic liquor; the Caryophyllus myrtle, of which the bark forms an esteemed cinnamon; the Eugenia Pimenta, from whence comes Jamaica pepper; the common myrtle, from whose buds and berries spice is sometimes made; the Eucalyptus manifera, which yields a sweet sort of manna; the Guinea Eucalyptus, the sap of which is transformed into beer by fermentation; in short, all those trees known under the name of gum-trees or iron-bark trees in Australia, belong to this family of the myrtaceæ, which contains forty-six genera and thirteen hundred species!"

The lad was allowed to run on, and he delivered his little

botanical lecture with great animation. Cyrus Harding listened smiling, and Pencroft with an indescribable feeling of pride.

"Very good, Herbert," replied Pencroft, "but I could swear that all those useful specimens you have just told us about are none of them giants like these!"

"That is true, Pencroft."

"That supports what I said," returned the sailor, "namely, that these giants are good for nothing!"

"There you are wrong, Pencroft," said the engineer; "these gigantic eucalypti, which shelter us, are good for something."

"And what is that?"

"To render the countries which they inhabit healthy. Do you know what they are called in Australia and New Zealand?"

"No, captain."

"They are called 'fever trees.'"

"Because they give fevers?"

"No, because they prevent them!"

"Good. I must note that," said the reporter.

"Note it then, my dear Spilett; for it appears proved that the presence of the eucalyptus is enough to neutralise miasmas. This natural antidote has been tried in certain countries in the middle of Europe and the north of Africa, where the soil was absolutely unhealthy, and the sanitary condition of the inhabitants has been gradually ameliorated. No more intermittent fevers prevail in the regions now covered with forests of the myrtaceæ. This fact is now beyond doubt, and it is a happy circumstance for us settlers in Lincoln Island."

"Ah! what an island! What a blessed island!" cried Pencroft. "I tell you, it wants nothing—unless it is—"

"That will come, Pencroft, that will be found," replied the engineer; "but now we must continue our voyage and push on as far as the river will carry our boat!"

The exploration was therefore continued for another two miles in the midst of country covered with eucalypti, which predominated in the woods of this portion of the island. The space which they occupied extended as far as the eye could reach on each side of the Mercy, which wound along between high green banks. The bed was often obstructed by long weeds, and even by pointed rocks, which rendered the navigation very difficult. The action of the oars was prevented, and Pencroft was obliged to push with a pole. They found also that the water was becoming shallower and shallower, and that the canoe must soon stop. The sun was already sinking towards the horizon, and the trees threw long shadows on the ground. Cyrus Harding, seeing that he could not hope to reach the western coast of the island in one journey, resolved to camp at the place where any further navigation was prevented by want of water. He calculated that they were still five or six miles from the coast, and this distance was too great for them to attempt traversing during the night in the midst of unknown woods.

The boat was pushed on through the forest, which gradually became thicker again, and appeared also to have more inhabitants; for if the eyes of the sailor did not deceive him, he thought he saw bands of monkeys springing among the trees. Sometimes even two or three of these animals stopped at a little distance from the canoe and gazed at the settlers without manifesting any terror, as if, seeing men for the first time, they had not yet learned to fear them. It would have been easy to bring down one of these quadrumani with a gunshot, and Pencroft was greatly tempted to fire, but Harding opposed so useless a massacre. This was prudent, for the monkeys, or apes rather, appearing to be very powerful and extremely active, it was useless to provoke an unnecessary aggression, and the creatures might, ignorant of the power of the explorer's firearms, have attacked them. It is true that the sailor considered the monkeys from a purely alimentary point of view, for those animals which are herbivorous make very excellent game; but since they had an abundant supply of provisions, it was a pity to waste their ammunition.

Towards four o'clock, the navigation of the Mercy became exceedingly difficult, for its course was obstructed by aquatic plants and rocks. The banks rose higher and higher, and already they were approaching the spurs of Mount Franklin. The source could not be far off, since it was fed by the water from the southern slopes of the mountain.

"In a quarter of an hour," said the sailor, "we shall be obliged to stop, captain."

"Very well, we will stop, Pencroft, and we will make our encampment for the night."

"At what distance are we from Granite House?" asked Herbert.

"About seven miles," replied the engineer, "taking into calculation, however, the *détours* of the river, which has carried us to the north-west."

"Shall, we go on?" asked the reporter.

"Yes, as long as we can," replied Cyrus Harding. "To-morrow, at break of day, we will leave the canoe, and in two hours I hope we shall cross the distance which separates us from the coast, and then we shall have the whole day in which to explore the shore."

"Go-ahead!" replied Pencroft.

But soon the boat grated on the stony bottom of the river, which was now not more than twenty feet in breadth. The trees met like a bower overhead, and caused a half-darkness. They also heard the noise of a waterfall, which showed that a few hundred feet up the river there was a natural barrier.

Presently, after a sudden turn of the river, a cascade appeared through the trees. The canoe again touched the bottom, and in a few minutes it was moored to a trunk near the right bank.

It was nearly five o'clock. The last rays of the sun gleamed through the thick foliage and glanced on the little waterfall, making the spray sparkle with all the colours of the rainbow. Beyond that, the Mercy was lost in the brushwood, where it was fed from some hidden source. The different streams which flowed into it increased it to a regular river further down, but here it was simply a shallow, limpid brook.

It was agreed to camp here, as the place was charming. The colonists disembarked, and a fire was soon lighted under a clump of trees, among the branches of which Cyrus Harding and his companions could, if it was necessary, take refuge for the night.

Supper was quickly devoured, for they were very hungry, and then there was only sleeping to think of. But, as roarings of rather a suspicious nature had been heard during the evening, a good fire was made up for the night, so as to protect the sleepers with its crackling flames. Neb and Pencroft also watched by turns, and did not spare fuel. They thought they saw the dark forms of some wild animals prowling round the camp among the bushes, but the night passed without incident, and the next day, the 31st of October, at five o'clock in the morning, all were on foot, ready for a start.

CHAPTER IV

Journey to the Coast—Troops of Monkeys—A new River—The Reason the Tide was not felt—A woody Shore—Reptile Promontory—Herbert envies Gideon Spilett—Explosion of Bamboos.

It was six o'clock in the morning when the settlers, after a hasty breakfast, set out to reach by the shortest way the western coast of the island. And how long would it take to do this? Cyrus Harding had said two hours, but of course that depended on the nature of the obstacles they might meet with. As it was probable that they would have to cut a path through the grass, shrubs, and creepers, they marched axe in hand, and with guns also ready, wisely taking warning from the cries of the wild beasts heard in the night.

The exact position of the encampment could be determined by the bearing of Mount Franklin, and as the volcano arose in the north at a distance of less than three miles, they had only to go straight towards the south-west to reach the western coast. They set out, having first carefully secured the canoe. Pencroft and Neb carried sufficient provisions for the little band for at least two days. It would not thus be necessary to hunt. The engineer advised his companions to refrain from firing, that their presence might not be betrayed to any one near the shore. The first hatchet blows were given among the brushwood in the midst of some mastick-trees, a little above the cascade; and his compass in his hand, Cyrus Harding led the way.

The forest here was composed for the most part of trees which had already been met with near the lake and on Prospect Heights. There were deodars, Douglas firs, casuarinas, gum-trees, eucalypti, hibiscus, cedars, and other trees, generally of a moderate size, for their number prevented their growth.

Since their departure, the settlers had descended the slopes which constituted the mountain system of the island, on to a dry soil, but the luxuriant vegetation of which indicated it to be watered either by some subterranean marsh or by some stream. However, Cyrus Harding did not remember to have seen, at the time of his excursion to the crater, any other watercourses but the Red Creek and the Mercy.

During the first part of their excursion, they saw numerous troops of monkeys who exhibited great astonishment at the sight of

25

men, whose appearance was so new to them. Gideon Spilett jokingly asked whether these active and merry quadrupeds did not consider him and his companions as degenerate brothers.

And certainly, pedestrians, hindered at each step by bushes, caught by creepers, barred by trunks of trees, did not shine beside those supple animals, who, bounding from branch to branch, were hindered by nothing on their course. The monkeys were numerous, but happily they did not manifest any hostile disposition.

Several pigs, agoutis, kangaroos, and other rodents were seen, also two or three kaolas, at which Pencroft longed to have a shot.

"But," said he, "you may jump and play just now; we shall have one or two words to say to you on our way back!"

At half-past nine the way was suddenly found to be barred by an unknown stream, from thirty to forty feet broad, whose rapid current dashed foaming over the numerous rocks which interrupted its course. This creek was deep and clear, but it was absolutely unnavigable.

"We are cut off!" cried Neb.

"No," replied Herbert, "it is only a stream, and we can easily swim over."

"What would be the use of that?" returned Harding. "This creek evidently runs to the sea. Let us remain on this side and follow the bank, and I shall be much astonished if it does not lead us very quickly to the coast. Forward!"

"One minute," said the reporter. "The name of this creek, my friends? Do not let us leave our geography incomplete."

"All right!" said Pencroft.

"Name it, my boy," said the engineer, addressing the lad.

"Will it not be better to wait until we have explored it to its mouth?" answered Herbert.

"Very well," replied Cyrus Harding. "Let us follow it as fast as we can without stopping."

"Still another minute!" said Pencroft.

"What's the matter?" asked the reporter.

"Though hunting is forbidden, fishing is allowed, I suppose," said the sailor.

"We have no time to lose," replied the engineer.

"Oh! five minutes!" replied Pencroft, "I only ask for five minutes to use in the interest of our breakfast!"

And Pencroft, lying down on the bank, plunged his arm into the water, and soon pulled up several dozen of fine crayfish from among the stores.

"These will be good!" cried Neb, going to the sailor's aid.

"As I said, there is everything in this island, except tobacco!" muttered Pencroft with a sigh.

The fishing did not take five minutes for the crayfish were swarming in the creek. A bag was filled with the crustaceæ, whose shells were of a cobalt blue. The settlers then pushed on.

They advanced more rapidly and easily along the bank of the river than in the forest. From time to time they came upon the traces of animals of a large size who had come to quench their thirst at the stream but none were actually seen and it was evidently not in this part of the forest that the peccary had received the bullet which had cost Pencroft a grinder.

In the meanwhile, considering the rapid current Harding was led to suppose that he and his companions were much farther from the western coast than they had at first supposed. In fact, at this hour, the rising tide would have turned back the current of the creek if its mouth had only been a few miles distant. Now, this effect was not produced, and the water pursued its natural course. The engineer was much astonished at this, and frequently consulted his compass to assure himself that some turn of the river was not leading them again into the Far West.

However, the creek gradually widened and its waters became less tumultuous. The trees on the right bank were as close together as on the left bank, and it was impossible to distinguish anything beyond them, but these masses of wood were evidently uninhabited, for Top did not bark, and the intelligent animal would not have failed to signal the presence of any stranger in the neighbourhood.

At half past ten, to the great surprise of Cyrus Harding, Herbert, who was a little in front, suddenly stopped and exclaimed—

"The sea!"

In a few minutes more, the whole western shore of the island lay extended before the eyes of the settlers.

But what a contrast between this and the eastern coast, upon which chance had first thrown them. No granite cliff, no rocks, not even a sandy beach. The forest reached the shore, and the tall trees bending over the water were beaten by the waves. It was not such a shore as is usually formed by nature, either by extending a vast carpet of sand, or by grouping masses of rock, but a beautiful border consisting of the most splendid trees. The bank was raised a little above the level of the sea, and on this luxuriant soil supported by a granite base, the fine forest trees seemed to be as firmly planted as in the interior of the island.

The colonists were then on the shore of an unimportant little harbour, which would scarcely have contained even two or three fishing boats. It served as a neck to the new creek of which the curious thing was that its waters, instead of joining the sea by a gentle slope, fell from a height of more than forty feet, which explained why the rising tide was not felt up the stream. In fact, the tides of the Pacific, even at their maximum of elevation, could never reach the level of the river, and, doubtless millions of years would pass before the water would have worn away the granite and hollowed a practicable mouth.

It was settled that the name of Falls River should be given to this stream. Beyond, towards the north, the forest border was prolonged for a space of nearly two miles, then the trees became scarcer, and beyond that again the picturesque heights described a nearly straight line which ran north and south. On the contrary, all the part of the shore between Falls River and Reptile End was a mass of wood, magnificent trees, some straight, others bent, so that the long sea swell bathed their roots. Now, it was this coast, that is, all the Serpentine peninsula, that was to be explored, for this part of the shore offered a refuge to castaways, which the other wild and barren side must have refused.

The weather was fine and clear, and from the height of a hillock on which Neb and Pencroft had arranged breakfast, a wide view was obtained. There was, however, not a sail in sight; nothing could be seen along the shore as far as the eye could reach. But the engineer would take nothing for granted until he had explored the coast to the very extremity of the Serpentine peninsula.

Breakfast was soon despatched, and at half-past eleven the captain gave the signal for departure. Instead of proceeding over the summit of a cliff or along a sandy beach, the settlers were obliged to remain under cover of the trees so that they might continue on the shore.

The distance which separated Falls River from Reptile End was about twelve miles. It would have taken the settlers four hours to do this, on a clear ground and without hurrying themselves; but as it was they needed double the time, for what with trees to go round, bushes to cut down, and creepers to chop away, they were impeded at every step, these obstacles greatly lengthening their journey.

There was, however, nothing to show that a shipwreck had taken place recently. It is true that, as Gideon Spilett observed, any remains of it might have drifted out to sea, and they must not take it for granted that because they could find no traces of it, a ship had not been cast away on the coast.

The reporter's argument was just, and besides, the incident of the bullet proved that a shot must have been fired in Lincoln Island within three months.

It was already five o'clock, and there were still two miles between the settlers and the extremity of the Serpentine peninsula. It was evident that after having reached Reptile End, Harding and his companions would not have time to return before dark to their encampment near the source of the Mercy. It would therefore be necessary to pass the night on the promontory. But they had no lack of provisions, which was lucky, for there were no animals on the shore, though birds, on the contrary, abounded—jacamars, couroucoos, tragopans, grouse, lories, parrots, cockatoos, pheasants, pigeons, and a hundred others. There was not a tree without a nest, and not a nest which was not full of flapping wings.

Towards seven o'clock the weary explorers arrived at Reptile End. Here the seaside forest ended, and the shore resumed the customary appearance of a coast, with rocks, reefs, and sands. It was possible that something might be found here, but darkness came on, and the further exploration had to be put off to the next day.

Pencroft and Herbert hastened on to find a suitable place for their camp. Amongst the last trees of the forest of the Far West, the boy found several thick clumps of bamboos.

"Good," said he; "this is a valuable discovery."

"Valuable?" returned Pencroft.

"Certainly," replied Herbert. "I may say, Pencroft, that the bark of the bamboo cut into flexible laths, is used for making baskets; that this bark, mashed into a paste, is used for the manufacture of Chinese paper; that the stalks furnish, according to their size, canes and pipes, and are used for conducting water; that large bamboos make excellent material for building, being light and strong, and being never attacked by insects. I will add that by sawing the bamboo in two at the joint, keeping for the bottom the part of the transverse film which forms the joint, useful cups are obtained, which are much in use among the Chinese. No! you don't care for that. But—"

"But what?"

"But I can tell you, if you are ignorant of it, that in India these bamboos are eaten like asparagus."

"Asparagus thirty feet high!" exclaimed the sailor. "And are they good?"

"Excellent," replied Herbert. "Only it is not the stems of thirty feet high which are eaten, but the young shoots."

29

"Perfect, my boy, perfect!" replied Pencroft.

"I will also add that the pith of the young stalks, preserved in vinegar, makes a good pickle."

"Better and better, Herbert!"

"And lastly, that the bamboos exude a sweet liquor which can be made into a very agreeable drink."

"Is that all?" asked the sailor.

"That is all!"

"And they don't happen to do for smoking?"

"No, my poor Pencroft."

Herbert and the sailor had not to look long for a place in which to pass the night. The rocks, which must have been violently beaten by the sea under the influence of the winds of the south west, presented many cavities in which shelter could be found against the night air. But just as they were about to enter one of these caves a loud roaring arrested them.

"Back!" cried Pencroft. "Our guns are only loaded with small shot, and beasts which can roar as loud as that would care no more for it than for grams of salt!". And the sailor, seizing Herbert by the arm, dragged him behind a rock, just as a magnificent animal showed itself at the entrance of the cavern.

It was a jaguar of a size at least equal to its Asiatic congeners, that is to say, it measured five feet from the extremity of its head to the beginning of its tail. The yellow colour of its hair was relieved by streaks and regular oblong spots of black, which contrasted with the white of its chest. Herbert recognised it as the ferocious rival of the tiger, as formidable as the puma, which is the rival of the largest wolf!

The jaguar advanced and gazed around him with blazing eyes, his hair bristling as if this was not the first time he had scented man.

At this moment the reporter appeared round a rock, and Herbert, thinking that he had not seen the jaguar, was about to rush towards him, when Gideon Spilett signed to him to remain where he was. This was not his first tiger, and advancing to within ten feet of the animal he remained motionless, his gun to his shoulder, without moving a muscle. The jaguar collected itself for a spring, but at that moment a shot struck it in the eyes, and it fell dead.

Herbert and Pencroft rushed towards the jaguar. Neb and Harding also ran up, and they remained for some instants contemplating the animal as it lay stretched on the ground, thinking that its magnificent skin would be a great ornament to the hall at Granite House.

"Oh, Mr. Spilett, how I admire and envy you!" cried Herbert, in a fit of very natural enthusiasm.

"Well, my boy," replied the reporter, "you could have done the same."

"I! with such coolness!—"

"Imagine to yourself, Herbert, that the jaguar is only a hare, and you would fire as quietly as possible."

"That is," rejoined Pencroft, "it is not more dangerous than a hare!"

"And now," said Gideon Spilett, "since the jaguar has left its abode, I do not see, my friends, why we should not take possession of it for the night."

"But others may come," said Pencroft.

"It will be enough to light a fire at the entrance of the cavern," said the reporter, "and no wild beasts will dare to cross the threshold."

"Into the jaguar's house, then!" replied the sailor, dragging after him the body of the animal.

Whilst Neb skinned the jaguar, his companions collected an abundant supply of dry wood from the forest, which they heaped up at the cave.

Cyrus Harding, seeing the clump of bamboos, cut a quantity, which he mingled with the other fuel.

This done, they entered the grotto, of which the floor was strewn with bones, the guns were carefully loaded, in case of a sudden attack, they had supper, and then just before they lay down to rest, the heap of wood piled at the entrance was set fire to. Immediately, a regular explosion, or rather, a series of reports, broke the silence! The noise was caused, by the bamboos, which, as the flames reached them, exploded like fireworks. The noise was enough to terrify even the boldest of wild beasts.

It was not the engineer who had invented this way of causing loud explosions, for, according to Marco Polo, the Tartars have employed it for many centuries to drive away from their encampments the formidable wild beasts of Central Asia.

CHAPTER V

Proposal to return by the Southern Shore—Configuration of the Coast—Searching for the supposed Wreck—A Wreck in the Air—Discovery of a small Natural Port—At Midnight on the Banks of the Mercy—The Canoe Adrift.

Cyrus Harding and his companions slept like innocent marmots in the cave which the jaguar had so politely left at their disposal.

At sunrise all were on the shore at the extremity of the promontory, and their gaze was directed towards the horizon, of which two-thirds of the circumference were visible. For the last time the engineer could ascertain that not a sail nor the wreck of a ship was on the sea, and even with the telescope nothing suspicious could be discovered.

There was nothing either on the shore, at least, in the straight line of three miles which formed the south side of the promontory, for beyond that, rising ground hid the rest of the coast, and even from the extremity of the Serpentine Peninsula Cape Claw could not be seen.

The southern coast of the island still remained to be explored. Now should they undertake it immediately, and devote this day to it?

This was not included in their first plan. In fact, when the boat was abandoned at the sources of the Mercy, it had been agreed that after having surveyed the west coast, they should go back to it, and return to Granite House by the Mercy. Harding then thought that the western coast would have offered refuge, either to a ship in distress, or to a vessel in her regular course; but now, as he saw that this coast presented no good anchorage, he wished to seek on the south what they had not been able to find on the west.

Gideon Spilett proposed to continue the exploration, that the question of the supposed wreck might be completely settled, and he asked at what distance Claw Cape might be from the extremity of the peninsula.

"About thirty miles," replied the engineer, "if we take into consideration the curvings of the coast."

"Thirty miles!" returned Spilett. "That would be a long day's march. Nevertheless, I think that we should return to Granite House by the south coast."

"But," observed Herbert, "from Claw Cape to Granite House there must be at least another ten miles."

"Make it forty miles in all," replied the engineer, "and do not hesitate to do it. At least we should survey the unknown shore, and then we shall not have to begin the exploration again."

"Very good," said Pencroft. "But the boat?"

"The boat has remained by itself for one day at the sources of the Mercy," replied Gideon Spilett; "it may just as well stay there two days! As yet, we have had no reason to think that the island is infested by thieves!"

"Yet," said the sailor, "when I remember the history of the turtle, I am far from confident of that."

"The turtle! the turtle!" replied the reporter. "Don't you know that the sea turned it over?"

"Who knows?" murmured the engineer.

"But—" said Neb.

Neb had evidently something to say, for he opened his mouth to speak and yet said nothing.

"What do you want to say, Neb?" asked the engineer.

"If we return by the shore to Claw Cape," replied Neb, "after having doubled the Cape, we shall be stopped—"

"By the Mercy! of course," replied Herbert, "and we shall have neither bridge nor boat by which to cross."

"But, captain," added Pencroft, "with a few floating trunks we shall have no difficulty in crossing the river."

"Never mind," said Spilett, "it will be useful to construct a bridge if we wish to have an easy access to the Far West!"

"A bridge!" cried Pencroft. "Well, is not the captain the best engineer in his profession? He will make us a bridge when we want one. As to transporting you this evening to the other side of the Mercy, and that without wetting one thread of your clothes, I will take care of that. We have provisions for another day, and besides we can get plenty of game. Forward!"

The reporter's proposal, so strongly seconded by the sailor, received general approbation, for each wished to have their doubts set at rest, and by returning by Claw Cape the exploration would be ended. But there was not an hour to lose, for forty miles was a long march, and they could not hope to reach Granite House before night.

At six o'clock in the morning the little band set out. As a precaution the guns were loaded with ball, and Top, who led the van, received orders to beat about the edge of the forest.

From the extremity of the promontory which formed the tail

33

of the peninsula the coast was rounded for a distance of five miles, which was rapidly passed over, without even the most minute investigations bringing to light the least trace of any old or recent landings; no *debris*, no mark of an encampment, no cinders of a fire, nor even a footprint!

From the point of the peninsula on which the settlers now were their gaze could extend along the south-west. Twenty-five miles off the coast terminated in the Claw Cape, which loomed dimly through the morning mists, and which, by the phenomenon of the mirage, appeared as if suspended between land and water.

Between the place occupied by the colonists and the other side of the immense bay, the shore was composed, first, of a tract of low land, bordered in the background by trees; then the shore became more irregular, projecting sharp points into the sea, and finally ended in the black rocks which, accumulated in picturesque disorder, formed Claw Cape.

Such was the development of this part of the island, which the settlers took in at a glance, whilst stopping for an instant.

"If a vessel ran in here," said Pencroft, "she would certainly be lost. Sandbanks and reefs everywhere! Bad quarters!"

"But at least something would be left of the ship," observed the reporter.

"There might be pieces of wood on the rocks, but nothing on the sands," replied the sailor.

"Why?"

"Because the sands are still more dangerous than the rocks, for they swallow up everything that is thrown on them. In a few days the hull of a ship of several hundred tons would disappear entirely in there!"

"So, Pencroft," asked the engineer, "if a ship has been wrecked on these banks, is it not astonishing that there is now no trace of her remaining?"

"No, captain, with the aid of time and tempest. However, it would be surprising, even in this case, that some of the masts or spars should not have been thrown on the beach, out of reach of the waves."

"Let us go on with our search, then," returned Cyrus Harding.

At one o'clock the colonists arrived at the other side of Washington Bay, they having now gone a distance of twenty miles.

They then halted for breakfast.

Here began the irregular coast, covered with lines of rocks and sandbanks. The long sea-swell could be seen breaking over the rocks in the bay, forming a foamy fringe. From this point to Claw Cape the beach was very narrow between the edge of the forest and the reefs.

Walking was now more difficult, on account of the numerous rocks which encumbered the beach. The granite cliff also gradually increased in height, and only the green tops of the trees which crowned it could be seen.

After half an hour's rest, the settlers resumed their journey, and not a spot among the rocks was left unexamined. Pencroft and Neb even rushed into the surf whenever any object attracted their attention. But they found nothing, some curious formations of the rocks having deceived them. They ascertained, however, that eatable shell-fish abounded there, but these could not be of any great advantage to them until some easy means of communication had been established between the two banks of the Mercy, and until the means of transport had been perfected.

Nothing therefore which threw any light on the supposed wreck could be found on this shore, yet an object of any importance, such as the hull of a ship, would have been seen directly, or any of her masts and spars would have been washed on shore, just as the chest had been, which was found twenty miles from here. But there was nothing.

Towards three o'clock Harding and his companions arrived at a snug little creek. It formed quite a natural harbour, invisible from the sea, and was entered by a narrow channel. At the back of this creek some violent convulsion had torn up the rocky border, and a cutting, by a gentle slope, gave access to an upper plateau, which might be situated at least ten miles from Claw Cape, and consequently four miles in a straight line from Prospect Heights. Gideon Spilett proposed to his companions that they should make a halt here. They agreed readily, for their walk had sharpened their appetites; and although it was not their usual dinner-hour, no one refused to strengthen himself with a piece of venison. This luncheon would sustain them till their supper, which they intended to take at Granite House. In a few minutes the settlers, seated under a clump of fine sea-pines, were devouring the provisions which Neb produced from his bag.

This spot was raised from fifty to sixty feet above the level of the sea. The view was very extensive, but beyond the cape it ended in Union Bay. Neither the islet nor Prospect Heights were visible, and could not be from thence, for the rising ground and the curtain of trees closed the northern horizon.

It is useless to add that notwithstanding the wide extent of sea which the explorers could survey, and though the engineer swept the horizon with his glass, no vessel could be found.

The shore was of course examined with the same care from the edge of the water to the cliff, and nothing could be discovered even with the aid of the instrument.

"Well," said Gideon Spilett, "it seems we must make up our minds to console ourselves with thinking that no one will come to dispute with us the possession of Lincoln Island!"

"But the bullet," cried Herbert. "That was not imaginary, I suppose!"

"Hang it, no!" exclaimed Pencroft, thinking of his absent tooth.

"Then what conclusion may be drawn?" asked the reporter.

"This," replied the engineer, "that three months or more ago, a vessel, either voluntarily or not, came here."

"What! then you admit, Cyrus, that she was swallowed up without leaving any trace?" cried the reporter.

"No, my dear Spilett, but you see that if it is certain that a human being set foot on the island, it appears no less certain that he has now left it."

"Then, if I understand you right, captain," said Herbert, "the vessel has left again?"

"Evidently."

"And we have lost an opportunity to get back to our country?" said Neb.

"I fear so."

"Very well, since the opportunity is lost, let us go on, it can't be helped," said Pencroft, who felt home sickness for Granite House.

But just as they were rising, Top was heard loudly barking; and the dog issued from the wood, holding in his mouth a rag soiled with mud.

Neb seized it. It was a piece of strong cloth!

Top still barked, and by his going and coming, seemed to invite his master to follow him into the forest.

"Now there's something to explain the bullet!" exclaimed Pencroft.

"A castaway!" replied Herbert.

"Wounded, perhaps!" said Neb.

"Or dead!" added the reporter.

All ran after the dog, among the tall pines on the border of the forest. Harding and his companions made ready their fire-arms, in case of an emergency.

They advanced some way into the wood, but to their great disappointment, they as yet saw no signs of any human being having passed that way. Shrubs and creepers were uninjured, and they had even to cut them away with the axe, as they had done in the deepest recesses of the forest. It was difficult to fancy that any human creature had ever passed there, but yet Top went backwards and forwards, not like a dog who searches at random, but like a being endowed with a mind, who is following up an idea.

In about seven or eight minutes Top stopped in a glade surrounded with tall trees. The settlers gazed around them, but saw nothing, neither under the bushes nor among the trees.

"What is the matter, Top?" said Cyrus Harding.

Top barked louder, bounding about at the foot of a gigantic pine. All at once Pencroft shouted,—

"Ho, splendid! capital!"

"What is it?" asked Spilett

"We have been looking for a wreck at sea or on land!"

"Well?"

"Well, and here we've found one in the air!"

And the sailor pointed to a great white rag, caught in the top of a pine, a fallen scrap of which the dog had brought to them.

"But that is not a wreck!" cried Gideon Spilett.

"I beg your pardon!" returned Pencroft.

"Why? is it—?"

"It is all that remains of our airy boat, of our balloon, which has been caught up aloft there, at the top of that tree!"

Pencroft was not mistaken, and he gave vent to his feelings in a tremendous hurrah, adding,—

"There is good cloth! There is what will furnish us with linen for years. There is what will make us handkerchiefs and shirts! Ha, ha, Mr Spilett, what do you say to an island where shirts grow on the trees?"

It was certainly a lucky circumstance for the settlers in Lincoln Island that the balloon, after having made its last bound into the air, had fallen on the island and thus given them the opportunity of finding it again, whether they kept the case under its present form, or whether they wished to attempt another escape by it, or whether they usefully employed the several hundred yards of cotton, which was of fine quality. Pencroft's joy was therefore shared by all.

But it was necessary to bring down the remains of the balloon from the tree, to place it in security, and this was no slight task.

Neb, Herbert, and the sailor, climbing to the summit of the tree, used all their skill to disengage the now reduced balloon.

The operation lasted two hours, and then not only the case, with its valve, its springs, its brasswork, lay on the ground, but the net, that is to say a considerable quantity of ropes and cordage, and the circle and the anchor. The case, except for the fracture, was in good condition, only the lower portion being torn.

It was a fortune which had fallen from the sky. "All the same, captain," said the sailor, "if we ever decide to leave the island, it won't be in a balloon, will it? These air-boats won't go where we want them to go, and we have had some experience in that way! Look here, We will build a craft of some twenty tons, and then we can make a main-sail, a fore-sail, and a jib out of that cloth. As to the rest of it, that will help to dress us."

"We shall see, Pencroft," replied Cyrus Harding; "we shall see."

"In the meantime, we must put it in a safe place," said Neb.

They certainly could not think of carrying this load of cloth, ropes, and cordage, to Granite House, for the weight of it was very considerable, and whilst waiting for a suitable vehicle in which to convey it, it was of importance that this treasure should not be left longer exposed to the mercies of the first storm. The settlers uniting their efforts managed to drag it as far as the shore, where they discovered a large rocky cavity, which owing to its position could not be visited either by the wind or rain.

"We needed a locker, and now we have one," said Pencroft; "but as we cannot lock it up, it will be prudent to hide the opening. I don't mean from two-legged thieves, but; from those with four paws!"

At six o'clock, all was stowed away, and after having given the creek the very suitable name of "Port Balloon," the settlers pursued their way along Claw Cape. Pencroft and the engineer talked of the different projects which it was agreed to put into execution with the briefest possible delay. It was necessary first of all to throw a bridge over the Mercy, so as to establish an easy communication with the south of the island; then the cart must be taken to bring back the balloon, for the canoe alone could not carry it, then they would build a decked boat, and Pencroft would rig it as a cutter, and they would be able to undertake voyages of circumnavigation round the island, etc.

In the meanwhile night came on, and it was already dark when the settlers reached Flotsam Point, the place where they had discovered the precious chest.

The distance between Flotsam Point and Granite House was another four miles, and it was midnight when, after having followed the shore to the mouth of the Mercy, the settlers arrived at the first angle formed by the Mercy.

There the river was eighty feet in breadth, which was awkward to cross, but as Pencroft had taken upon himself to conquer this difficulty, he was compelled to do it. The settlers certainly had reason to be pretty tired. The journey had been long, and the task of getting down the balloon had not rested either their arms or legs. They were anxious to reach Granite House to eat and sleep, and if the bridge had been constructed, in a quarter of an hour they would have been at home.

The night was very dark. Pencroft prepared to keep his promise by constructing a sort of raft, on which to make the passage of the Mercy. He and Neb, armed with axes, chose two trees near the water, and began to attack them at the base.

Cyrus Harding and Spilett, seated on the bank, waited till their companions were ready for their help, whilst Herbert roamed about, though without going to any distance. All at once, the lad, who had strolled by the river, came running back, and, pointing up the Mercy, exclaimed,—

"What is floating there?"

Pencroft stopped working, and seeing an indistinct object moving through the gloom,—

"A canoe!" cried he.

All approached, and saw to their extreme surprise, a boat floating down the current.

"Boat ahoy!" shouted the sailor, without thinking that perhaps it would be best to keep silence.

No reply. The boat still drifted onwards, and it was not more than twelve feet off, when the sailor exclaimed—

"But it is our own boat! she has broken her moorings, and floated down the current. I must say she has arrived very opportunely."

"Our boat?" murmured the engineer.

Pencroft was right. It was indeed the canoe, of which the rope had undoubtedly broken, and which had come alone from the sources of the Mercy. It was very important to seize it before the rapid current should have swept it away out of the mouth of the river, but Neb and Pencroft cleverly managed this by means of a long pole.

The canoe touched the shore. The engineer leapt in first, and

39

found, on examining the rope, that it had been really worn through by rubbing against the rocks.

"Well," said the reporter to him, in a low voice, "this is a strange thing."

"Strange indeed!" returned Cyrus Handing.

Strange or not, it was very fortunate. Herbert, the reporter, Neb, and Pencroft, embarked in turn. There was no doubt about the rope having been worn through, but the astonishing part of the affair was, that the boat should have arrived just at the moment when the settlers were there to seize it on its way, for a quarter of an hour earlier or later it would have been lost in the sea.

If they had been living in the time of genii, this incident would have given them the right to think that the island was haunted by some supernatural being, who used his power in the service of the castaways!

A few strokes of the oar brought the settlers to the mouth of the Mercy. The canoe was hauled up on the beach near the Chimneys, and all proceeded towards the ladder of Granite House.

But at that moment, Top barked angrily, and Neb, who was looking for the first steps, uttered a cry.

There was no longer a ladder!

CHAPTER VI

**Pencroft's Halloos—A Night in the Chimneys—
Herbert's Arrows—The Captain's Project—An unexpected
Explanation—What has happened in Granite House—How
a new Servant enters the Service of the Colonists.**

Cyrus Harding stood still, without saying a word. His
companions searched in the darkness on the wall, in case the wind
should have moved the ladder, and on the ground, thinking that it
might have fallen down.... But the ladder had quite disappeared. As
to ascertaining if a squall had blown it on to the landing-place, half
way up, that was impossible in the dark.

"If it is a joke," cried Pencroft, "it is a very stupid one; to come
home and find no staircase to go up to your room by; for weary
men, there is nothing to laugh at that I can see."

Neb could do nothing but cry out, "Oh! oh! oh!"

"I begin to think that very curious things happen in Lincoln
Island!" said Pencroft.

"Curious?" replied Gideon Spilett, "not at all, Pencroft,
nothing can be more natural. Some one has come during our
absence, taken possession of our dwelling and drawn up the ladder."

"Some one," cried the sailor. "But who?"

"Who but the hunter who fired the bullet?" replied the
reporter.

"Well, if there is any one up there," replied Pencroft, who
began to lose patience, "I will give them a hail, and they must
answer."

And in a stentorian voice the sailor gave a prolonged "Halloo!"
which was echoed again and again from the cliff and rocks.

The settlers listened and they thought they heard a sort of
chuckling laugh, of which they could not guess the origin. But no
voice replied to Pencroft, who in vain repeated his vigorous shouts.

There was something indeed in this to astonish the most
apathetic of men, and the settlers were not men of that description.
In their situation every incident had its importance, and, certainly,
during the seven months which they had spent on the island, they
had not before met with anything of so surprising a character.

Be that as it may, forgetting their fatigue in the singularity of
the event, they remained below Granite House, not knowing what to
think, not knowing what to do, questioning each other without any
hope of a satisfactory reply, every one starting some supposition

41

each more unlikely than the last. Neb bewailed himself, much disappointed at not being able to get into his kitchen, for the provisions which they had had on their expedition were exhausted, and they had no means of renewing them.

"My friends," at last said Cyrus Harding, "there is only one thing to be done at present, wait for day, and then act according to circumstances. But let us go to the Chimneys. There we shall be under shelter, and if we cannot eat, we can at least sleep."

"But who is it that has played us this cool trick?" again asked Pencroft, unable to make up his mind to retire from the spot.

Whoever it was, the only thing practicable was to do as the engineer proposed, to go to the Chimneys and there wait for day. In the meanwhile Top was ordered to mount guard below the windows of Granite House, and when Top received an order he obeyed it without any questioning. The brave dog therefore remained at the foot of the cliff whilst his master with his companions sought a refuge among the rocks.

To say that the settlers, notwithstanding their fatigue, slept well on the sandy floor of the Chimneys would not be true. It was not only that they were extremely anxious to find out the cause of what had happened, whether it was the result of an accident which would be discovered at the return of day, or whether on the contrary it was the work of a human being; but they also had very uncomfortable beds. That could not be helped, however, for in some way or other at that moment their dwelling was occupied, and they could not possibly enter it.

Now Granite House was more than their dwelling, it was their warehouse. There were all the stores belonging to the colony, weapons, instruments, tools, ammunition, provisions, etc. To think that all that might be pillaged and that the settlers would have all their work to do over again, fresh weapons and tools to make, was a serious matter. Their uneasiness led one or other of them also to go out every few minutes to see if Top was keeping good watch. Cyrus Harding alone waited with his habitual patience, although his strong mind was exasperated at being confronted with such an inexplicable fact, and he was provoked at himself for allowing a feeling to which he could not give a name, to gain an influence over him. Gideon Spilett shared his feelings in this respect, and the two conversed together in whispers of the inexplicable circumstance which baffled even their intelligence and experience.

"It is a joke," said Pencroft; "it is a trick some one has played us. Well, I don't like such jokes, and the joker had better look out for himself, if he falls into my hands, I can tell him."

As soon as the first gleam of light appeared in the east, the colonists, suitably armed, repaired to the beach under Granite House. The rising sun now shone on the cliff and they could see the windows, the shutters of which were closed, through the curtains of foliage.

All here was in order; but a cry escaped the colonists when they saw that the door, which they had closed on their departure, was now wide open.

Some one had entered Granite House—there could be no more doubt about that.

The upper ladder, which generally hung from the door to the landing, was in its place, but the lower ladder was drawn up and raised to the threshold. It was evident that the intruders had wished to guard themselves against a surprise.

Pencroft hailed again.

No reply.

"The beggars," exclaimed the sailor. "There they are sleeping quietly as if they were in their own house. Hallo there, you pirates, brigands, robbers, sons of John Bull!".

When Pencroft, being a Yankee, treated any one to the epithet of "son of John Bull," he considered he had reached the last limits of insult.

The sun had now completely risen, and the whole façade of Granite House became illuminated by his rays; but in the interior as well as on the exterior all was quiet and calm.

The settlers asked if Granite House was inhabited or not, and yet the position of the ladder was sufficient to show that it was; it was also certain that the inhabitants, whoever they might be, had not been able to escape. But how were they to be got at?

Herbert then thought of fastening a cord to an arrow, and shooting the arrow so that it should pass between the first rounds of the ladder which hung from the threshold. By means of the cord they would then be able to draw down the ladder to the ground, and so re-establish the communication between the beach and Granite House. There was evidently nothing else to be done, and, with a little skill, this method might succeed. Very fortunately bows and arrows had been left at the Chimneys, where they also found a quantity of light hibiscus cord. Pencroft fastened this to a well-feathered arrow. Then Herbert fixing it to his bow, took a careful aim for the lower part of the ladder.

Cyrus Harding, Gideon Spilett, Pencroft, and Neb drew back, so as to see if anything appeared at the windows. The reporter lifted his gun to his shoulder and covered the door.

43

The bow was bent, the arrow flew, taking the cord with it, and passed between the two last rounds.

The operation had succeeded.

Herbert immediately seized the end of the cord, but, at that moment when he gave it a pull to bring down the ladder, an arm, thrust suddenly out between the wall and the door, grasped it and dragged it inside Granite House.

"The rascals!" shouted the sailor. "If a ball can do anything for you, you shall not have long to wait for it."

"But who was it?" asked Neb.

"Who was it? Didn't you see?"

"No."

"It was a monkey, a sapago, an orang-outang, a baboon, a gorilla, a sagoin. Our dwelling has been invaded by monkeys, who climbed up the ladder during our absence."

And, at this moment, as if to bear witness to the truth of the sailors words, two or three quadrumana showed themselves at the windows, from which they had pushed back the shutters, and saluted the real proprietors of the place with a thousand hideous grimaces.

"I knew that it was only a joke," cried Pencroft, "but one of the jokers shall pay the penalty for the rest."

So saying, the sailor, raising his piece, took a rapid aim at one of the monkeys and fired. All disappeared, except one who fell mortally wounded on the beach. This monkey, which was of a large size, evidently belonged to the first order of the quadrumana. Whether this was a chimpanzee, an orang-outang, or a gorilla, he took rank among the anthropoid apes, who are so called from their resemblance to the human race. However, Herbert declared it to be an orang-outang.

"What a magnificent beast!" cried Neb.

"Magnificent, if you like," replied Pencroft; "but still I do not see how we are to get into our house."

"Herbert is a good marksman," said the reporter, "and his bow is here. He can try again."

"Why, these apes are so cunning," returned Pencroft, "they won't show themselves again at the windows and so we can't kill them, and when I think of the mischief they may do in the rooms and storehouse—"

"Have patience," replied Harding; "these creatures cannot keep us long at bay."

"I shall not be sure of that till I see them down here," replied

44

the sailor "And now, captain, do you know how many dozens of these fellows are up there?"

It was difficult to reply to Pencroft, and as for the young boy making another attempt, that was not easy; for the lower part of the ladder had been drawn again into the door, and when another pull was given, the line broke and the ladder remained firm. The case was really perplexing. Pencroft stormed. There was a comic side to the situation, but he did not think it funny at all. It was certain that the settlers would end by reinstating themselves in their domicile and driving out the intruders, but when and how? that is what they were not able to say.

Two hours passed, during which the apes took care not to show themselves, but they were still there, and three or four times a nose or a paw was poked out at the door or windows, and was immediately saluted by a gun-shot.

"Let us hide ourselves," at last said the engineer. "Perhaps the apes will think we have gone quite away and will show themselves again. Let Spilett and Herbert conceal themselves behind those rocks and fire on all that may appear."

The engineer's orders were obeyed, and whilst the reporter and the lad, the best marksmen in the colony, posted themselves in a good position, but out of the monkeys' sight, Neb, Pencroft, and Cyrus climbed the plateau and entered the forest in order to kill some game, for it was now time for breakfast and they had no provisions remaining.

In half an hour the hunters returned with a few rock pigeons, which they roasted as well as they could. Not an ape had appeared. Gideon Spilett and Herbert went to take their share of the breakfast, leaving Top to watch under the windows. They then, having eaten, returned to their post.

Two hours later, their situation was in no degree improved. The quadrumana gave no sign of existence, and it might have been supposed that they had disappeared; but what seemed more probable was that, terrified by the death of one of their companions, and frightened by the noise of the firearms, they had retreated to the back part of the house or probably even into the storeroom. And when they thought of the valuables which this storeroom contained, the patience so much recommended by the engineer, fast changed into great irritation, and there certainly was room for it.

"Decidedly it is too bad," said the reporter; "and the worst of it is, there is no way of putting an end to it."

"But we must drive these vagabonds out somehow," cried the sailor. "We could soon get the better of them, even if there are

45

twenty of the rascals; but for that, we must meet them hand to hand. Come now, is there no way of getting at them?"

"Let us try to enter Granite House by the old opening at the lake," replied the engineer.

"Oh!" shouted the sailor, "and I never thought of that."

This was in reality the only way by which to penetrate into Granite House so as to fight with and drive out the intruders. The opening was, it is true, closed up with a wall of cemented stones, which it would be necessary to sacrifice, but that could easily be rebuilt. Fortunately, Cyrus Harding had not as yet effected his project of hiding this opening by raising the waters of the lake, for the operation would then have taken some time.

It was already past twelve o'clock when the colonists, well armed and provided with picks and spades, left the Chimneys, passed beneath the windows of Granite House, after telling Top to remain at his post, and began to ascend the left bank of the Mercy, so as to reach Prospect Heights.

But they had not made fifty steps in this direction, when they heard the dog barking furiously.

And all rushed down the bank again.

Arrived at the turning, they saw that the situation had changed.

In fact, the apes, seized with a sudden panic, from some unknown cause, were trying to escape. Two or three ran and clambered from one window to another with the agility of acrobats. They were not even trying to replace the ladder, by which it would have been easy to descend; perhaps in their terror they had forgotten this way of escape. The colonists, now being able to take aim without difficulty, fired. Some, wounded or killed, fell back into the rooms, uttering piercing cries. The rest, throwing themselves out, were dashed to pieces in their fall, and in a few minutes, so far as they knew, there was not a living quadrumana in Granite House.

At this moment the ladder was seen to slip over the threshold, then unroll and fall to the ground.

"Hullo!" cried the sailor, "this is queer!"

"Very strange!" murmured the engineer, leaping first up the ladder.

"Take care, captain!" cried Pencroft, "perhaps there are still some of these rascals..."

"We shall soon see," replied the engineer, without stopping however.

All his companions followed him, and in a minute they had arrived at the threshold. They searched everywhere. There was no one in the rooms nor in the storehouse, which had been respected by the band of quadrumana.

"Well now, and the ladder," cried the sailor; "who can the gentleman have been who sent us that down?"

But at that moment a cry was heard, and a great orang, who had hidden himself in the passage, rushed into the room, pursued by Neb.

"Ah the robber!" cried Pencroft.

And hatchet in hand, he was about to cleave the head of the animal, when Cyrus Harding seized his arm, saying,—

"Spare him, Pencroft."

"Pardon this rascal?"

"Yes! it was he who threw us the ladder!"

And the engineer said this in such a peculiar voice that it was difficult to know whether he spoke seriously or not.

Nevertheless, they threw themselves on the orang, who defended himself gallantly, but was soon overpowered and bound.

"There!" said Pencroft. "And what shall we make of him, now we've got him?"

"A servant!" replied Herbert.

The lad was not joking in saying this, for he knew how this intelligent race could be turned to account.

The settlers then approached the ape and gazed at it attentively. He belonged to the family of anthropoid apes, of which the facial angle is not much inferior to that of the Australians and Hottentots. It was an orang-outang, and as such, had neither the ferocity of the gorilla, nor the stupidity of the baboon. It is to this family of the anthropoid apes that so many characteristics belong which prove them to be possessed of an almost human intelligence. Employed in houses, they can wait at table, sweep rooms, brush clothes, clean boots, handle a knife, fork, and spoon properly, and even drink wine,... doing everything as well as the best servant that ever walked upon two legs. Buffon possessed one of these apes, who served him for a long time as a faithful and zealous servant.

The one which had been seized in the hall of Granite House was a great fellow, six feet high, with an admirably proportioned frame, a broad chest, head of a moderate size, the facial angle reaching sixty-five degrees, round skull, projecting nose, skin covered with soft glossy hair, in short, a fine specimen of the anthropoids. His eyes, rather smaller than human eyes, sparkled with intelligence, his white teeth glittered under his moustache, and he wore a little curly brown beard.

47

"A handsome fellow!" said Pencroft; "if we only knew his language, we could talk to him."

"But, master," said Neb, "are you serious? Are we going to take him as a servant?"

"Yes, Neb," replied the engineer, smiling. "But you must not be jealous."

"And I hope he will make an excellent servant," added Herbert. "He appears young, and will be easy to educate, and we shall not be obliged to use force to subdue him, nor draw his teeth, as is sometimes done. He will soon grow fond of his masters if they are kind to him."

"And they will be," replied Pencroft, who had forgotten all his rancour against "the jokers."

Then, approaching the orang,—

"Well, old boy!" he asked, "how are you?"

The orang replied by a little grunt which did not show any anger.

"You wish to join the colony?" again asked the sailor. "You are going to enter the service of Captain Cyrus Harding?"

Another respondent grunt was uttered by the ape.

"And you will be satisfied with no other wages than your food?"

Third affirmative grunt.

"This conversation is slightly monotonous," observed Gideon Spilett.

"So much the better," replied Pencroft, "the best servants are those who talk the least. And then, no wages, do you hear, my boy? We will give you no wages at first, but we will double them afterwards if we are pleased with you."

Thus the colony was increased by a new member. As to his name the sailor begged that in memory of another ape which he had known, he might be called Jupiter, and Jup for short.

And so, without more ceremony, Master Jup was installed in Granite House.

CHAPTER VII

Plans—A Bridge over the Mercy—Mode adopted for making an Island of Prospect Heights—The Drawbridge—Harvest—The Stream—The Poultry Yard—A Pigeon-house—The two Onagas—The Cart—Excursion to Port Balloon

The settlers in Lincoln Island had now regained their dwelling, without having been obliged to reach it by the old opening, and were therefore spared the trouble of mason's work. It was certainly lucky, that at the moment they were about to set out to do so, the apes had been seized with that terror, no less sudden than inexplicable, which had driven them out of Granite House. Had the animals discovered that they were about to be attacked from another direction? This was the only explanation of their sudden retreat.

During the day the bodies of the apes were carried into the wood, where they were buried; then the settlers busied themselves in repairing the disorder caused by the intruders, disorder but not damage, for although they had turned everything in the rooms topsy-turvy, yet they had broken nothing. Neb relighted his stove, and the stores in the larder furnished a substantial repast, to which all did ample justice.

Jup was not forgotten, and he ate with relish some stone-pine almonds and rhizome roots, with which he was abundantly supplied. Pencroft had unfastened his arms, but judged it best to have his legs tied until they were more sure of his submission.

Then, before retiring to rest, Harding and his companions seated round their table, discussed those plans, the execution of which was most pressing. The most important and most urgent was the establishment of a bridge over the Mercy, so as to form a communication with the southern part of the island and Granite House; then the making of an enclosure for the musmons or other woolly animals which they wished to capture.

These two projects would help to solve the difficulty as to their clothing, which was now serious. The bridge would render easy the transport of the balloon case, which would furnish them with linen, and the inhabitants of the enclosure would yield wool which would supply them with winter clothes.

As to the enclosure, it was Cyrus Harding's intention to establish it at the sources of the Red Creek, where the ruminants

49

would find fresh and abundant pasture. The road between Prospect Heights and the sources of the stream was already partly beaten, and with a better cart than the first, the material could be easily conveyed to the spot, especially if they could manage to capture some animals to draw it.

But though there might be no inconvenience in the enclosure being so far from Granite House, it would not be the same with the poultry-yard, to which Neb called the attention of the colonists. It was indeed necessary that the birds should be close within reach of the cook, and no place appeared more favourable for the establishment of the said poultry-yard than that portion of the banks of the lake which was close to the old opening.

Water-birds would prosper there as well as others, and the couple of tinamous taken in their last excursion would be the first to be domesticated.

The next day, the 3rd of November, the new works were begun by the construction of the bridge, and all hands were required for this important task. Saws, hatchets, and hammers were shouldered by the settlers, who, now transformed into carpenters, descended to the shore.

There Pencroft observed,—

"Suppose, that during our absence, Master Jup takes it into his head to draw up the ladder which he so politely returned to us yesterday?"

"Let us tie its lower end down firmly," replied Cyrus Harding.

This was done by means of two stakes securely fixed in the sand. Then the settlers, ascending the left bank of the Mercy, soon arrived at the angle formed by the river.

There they halted, in order to ascertain if the bridge could be thrown across. The place appeared suitable.

In fact, from this spot, to Port Balloon, discovered the day before on the southern coast, there was only a distance of three miles and a half, and from the bridge to the Port, it would be easy to make a good cart-road which would render the communication between Granite House and the south of the island extremely easy.

Cyrus Harding now imparted to his companions a scheme for completely isolating Prospect Heights so as to shelter it from the attacks both of quadrupeds and quadrumana. In this way, Granite House, the Chimneys, the poultry-yard, and all the upper part of the plateau which was to be used for cultivation, would be protected against the depredations of animals. Nothing could be easier than to execute this project, and this is how the engineer intended to set to work.

The plateau was already defended on three sides by watercourses, either artificial or natural. On the north-west, by the shores of Lake Grant, from the entrance of the passage to the breach made in the banks of the lake for the escape of the water.

On the north, from this breach to the sea, by the new watercourse which had hollowed out a bed for itself across the plateau and shore, above and below the fall, and it would be enough to dig the bed of this creek a little deeper to make it impracticable for animals, on all the eastern border by the sea itself, from the mouth of the aforesaid creek to the mouth of the Mercy.

Lastly on the south, from the mouth to the turn of the Mercy where the bridge was to be established.

The western border of the plateau now remained between the turn of the river and the southern angle of the lake, a distance of about a mile, which was open to all comers. But nothing could be easier than to dig a broad deep ditch, which could be filled from the lake, and the overflow of which would throw itself by a rapid fall into the bed of the Mercy. The level of the lake would, no doubt, be somewhat lowered by this fresh discharge of its waters, but Cyrus Harding had ascertained that the volume of water in the Red Creek was considerable enough to allow of the execution of this project.

"So then," added the engineer, "Prospect Heights will become a regular island, being surrounded with water on all sides, and only communicating with the rest of our domain by the bridge which we are about to throw across the Mercy, the two little bridges already established above and below the fall; and, lastly, two other little bridges which must be constructed, one over the canal which I propose to dig, the other across to the left bank of the Mercy. Now, if these bridges can be raised at will, Prospect Heights will be guarded from any surprise."

The bridge was the most urgent work. Trees were selected, cut down, stripped of their branches, and cut into beams, joists, and planks. The end of the bridge which rested on the right bank of the Mercy was to be firm, but the other end on the left bank was to be movable, so that it might be raised by means of a counterpoise, as some canal bridges are managed.

This was certainly a considerable work, and though it was skilfully conducted, it took some time, for the Mercy at this place was eighty feet wide. It was therefore necessary to fix piles in the bed of the river so as to sustain the floor of the bridge and establish a pile-driver to act on the tops of these piles, which would thus form two arches and allow the bridge to support heavy loads.

Happily there was no want of tools with which to shape the

51

wood, nor of iron-work to make it firm, nor of the ingenuity of a man who had a marvellous knowledge of the work, nor lastly, the zeal of his companions, who in seven months had necessarily acquired great skill in the use of their tools; and it must be said that not the least skillful was Gideon Spilett, who in dexterity almost equalled the sailor himself. "Who would ever have expected so much from a newspaper man!" thought Pencroft.

The construction of the Mercy bridge lasted three weeks of regular hard work. They even breakfasted on the scene of their labours, and the weather being magnificent, they only returned to Granite House to sleep.

During this period it may be stated that Master Jup grew more accustomed to his new masters, whose movements he always watched with very inquisitive eyes. However, as a precautionary measure, Pencroft did not as yet allow him complete liberty, rightly wishing to wait until the limits of the plateau should be settled by the projected works. Top and Jup were good friends and played willingly together, but Jup did everything solemnly.

On the 20th of November the bridge was finished. The movable part, balanced by the counterpoise, swung easily, and only a slight effort was needed to raise it; between its hinge and the last cross-bar on which it rested when closed, there existed a space of twenty feet, which was sufficiently wide to prevent any animals from crossing.

The settlers now began to talk of fetching the balloon-case, which they were anxious to place in perfect security; but to bring it, it would be necessary to take a cart to Port Balloon, and consequently, necessary to beat a road through the dense forests of the Far West. This would take some time. Also, Neb and Pencroft having gone to examine into the state of things at Port Balloon, and reported that the stock of cloth would suffer no damage in the grotto where it was stored, it was decided that the work at Prospect Heights should not be discontinued.

"That," observed Pencroft, "will enable us to establish our poultry-yard under better conditions, since we need have no fear of visits from foxes nor the attacks of other beasts."

"Then," added Neb, "we can clear the plateau, and transplant wild plants to it."

"And prepare our second cornfield!" cried the sailor with a triumphant air.

In fact, the first cornfield sown with a single grain had prospered admirably, thanks to Pencroft's care. It had produced the ten ears foretold by the engineer, and each ear containing eighty grains, the colony found itself in possession of eight hundred grains, in six months, which promised a double harvest each year.

These eight hundred grains, except fifty, which were prudently reserved, were to be sown in a new field, but with no less care than was bestowed on the single grain.

The field was prepared, then surrounded with a strong palisade, high and pointed, which quadrupeds would have found difficulty in leaping. As to birds, some scarecrows, due to Pencroft's ingenious brain, were enough to frighten them. The seven hundred and fifty grains, deposited in very regular furrows, were then left for nature to do the rest.

On the 21st of November, Cyrus Harding began to plan the canal which was to close the plateau on the west, from the south angle of Lake Grant to the angle of the Mercy. There was there two or three feet of vegetable earth, and below that granite. It was therefore necessary to manufacture some more nitro glycerine, and the nitro glycerine did its accustomed work. In less than a fortnight a ditch twelve feet wide and six deep, was dug out in the hard ground of the plateau. A new trench was made by the same means in the rocky border of the lake forming a small stream, to which they gave the name of Creek Glycerine, and which was thus an affluent of the Mercy. As the engineer had predicted, the level of the lake was lowered, though very slightly. To complete the enclosure the bed of the stream on the beach was considerably enlarged, and the sand supported by means of stakes.

By the end of the first fortnight of December these works were finished, and Prospect Heights—that is to say, a sort of irregular pentagon having a perimeter of nearly four miles, surrounded by a liquid belt—was completely protected from depredators of every description.

During the month of December, the heat was very great. In spite of it however, the settlers continued their work, and as they were anxious to possess a poultry-yard they forthwith commenced it.

It is useless to say that since the enclosing of the plateau had been completed, Master Jup had been set at liberty. He did not leave his masters, and evinced no wish to escape. He was a gentle animal, though very powerful and wonderfully active. He was already taught to make himself useful by drawing loads of wood and carting away the stones which were extracted from the bed of Creek Glycerine.

The poultry yard occupied an area of two hundred square yards on the south eastern bank of the lake. It was surrounded by a palisade, and in it were constructed various shelters for the birds which were to populate it. These were simply built of branches and divided into compartments made ready for the expected guests.

The first were the two tinamous, which were not long in having a number of young ones; they had for companions half a dozen ducks, accustomed to the borders of the lake. Some belonged to the Chinese species, of which the wings open like a fan, and which by the brilliancy of their plumage rival the golden pheasants. A few days afterwards, Herbert snared a couple of gallinaceæ, with spreading tails composed of long feathers, magnificent alectors, which soon became tame. As to pelicans, kingfishers, water-hens, they came of themselves to the shores of the poultry-yard, and this little community, after some disputes, cooing, screaming, clucking, ended by settling down peacefully, and increased in encouraging proportion for the future use of the colony.

Cyrus Harding, wishing to complete his performance, established a pigeon-house in a corner of the poultry-yard. There he lodged a dozen of those pigeons which frequented the rocks of the plateau. These birds soon became accustomed to returning every evening to their new dwelling, and showed more disposition to domesticate themselves than their congeners, the wood-pigeons.

Lastly, the time had come for turning the balloon-case to use, by cutting it up to make shirts and other articles; for as to keeping it in its present form, and risking themselves in a balloon filled with gas, above a sea of the limits of which they had no idea, it was not to be thought of.

It was necessary to bring the case to Granite House, and the colonists employed themselves in rendering their heavy cart lighter and more manageable. But though they had a vehicle, the moving power was yet to be found.

But did there not exist in the island some animal which might supply the place of the horse, ass, or ox? That was the question.

"Certainly," said Pencroft, "a beast of burden would be very useful to us until the captain has made a steam cart, or even an engine, for some day we shall have a railroad from Granite House to Port Balloon, with a branch line to Mount Franklin!"

One day, the 23rd of December, Neb and Top were heard shouting and barking, each apparently trying who could make the most noise. The settlers, who were busy at the Chimneys, ran, fearing some vexatious incident.

What did they see? Two fine animals of a large size, who had imprudently ventured on the plateau, when the bridges were open. One would have said they were horses, or at least donkeys, male and female, of a fine shape, dove-coloured, the legs and tail white, striped with black on the head and neck. They advanced quietly without showing any uneasiness, and gazed at the men, in whom they could not as yet recognise their future masters.

"These are onagas!" cried Herbert, "animals something between the zebra and the conaga!"

"Why not donkeys?" asked Neb.

"Because they have not long ears, and their shape is more graceful!"

"Donkeys or horses," interrupted Pencroft, "they are 'moving powers,' as the captain would say, and as such must be captured!"

The sailor, without frightening the animals, crept through the grass to the bridge over Creek Glycerine, lowered it, and the onagas were prisoners.

Now, should they seize them with violence and master them by force? No. It was decided that for a few days they should be allowed to roam freely about the plateau, where there was an abundance of grass, and the engineer immediately began to prepare a stable near the poultry-yard, in which the onagas might find food, with a good litter, and shelter during the night.

This done, the movements of the two magnificent creatures were left entirely free, and the settlers avoided even approaching them so as to terrify them. Several times, however, the onagas appeared to wish to leave the plateau, too confined for animals accustomed to the plains and forests. They were then seen following the water-barrier which everywhere presented itself before them, uttering short neighs, then galloping through the grass, and becoming calmer, they would remain entire hours gazing at the woods, from which they were cut off for ever!

In the meantime harness of vegetable fibre had been manufactured, and some days after the capture of the onagas, not only the cart was ready, but a straight road, or rather a cutting, had been made through the forests of the Far West, from the angle of the Mercy to Port Balloon. The cart might then be driven there, and towards the end of December they tried the onagas for the first time.

Pencroft had already coaxed the animals to come and eat out of his hand, and they allowed him to approach without making any difficulty, but once harnessed they reared and could with difficulty be held in. However it was not long before they submitted to this new service, for the onaga, being less refractory than the zebra, is frequently put in harness in the mountainous regions of Southern

Africa, and it has even been acclimatised in Europe, under zones of a relative coolness.

On this day all the colony, except Pencroft who walked at the animals' heads, mounted the cart, and set out on the road to Port Balloon.

Of course they were jolted over the somewhat rough road, but the vehicle arrived without any accident, and was soon loaded with the case and rigging of the balloon.

At eight o'clock that evening the cart, after passing over the Mercy bridge, descended the left bank of the river, and stopped on the beach. The onagas being unharnessed, were thence led to their stable, and Pencroft before going to sleep gave vent to his feelings in a deep sigh of satisfaction that awoke all the echoes of Granite House.

CHAPTER VIII

Linen—Shoes of Seal-leather—Manufacture of Pyroxyle—Gardening—Fishing—Turtle-eggs— Improvement of Master Jup—The Corral—Musmon Hunt—New Animal and Vegetable Possessions— Recollections of their Native Land.

The first week of January was devoted to the manufacture of the linen garments required by the colony. The needles found in the box were used by sturdy if not delicate fingers, and we may be sure that what was sewn was sewn firmly.

There was no lack of thread, thanks to Cyrus Harding's idea of re-employing that which had been already used in the covering of the balloon. This with admirable patience was all unpicked by Gideon Spilett and Herbert, for Pencroft had been obliged to give this work up, as it irritated him beyond measure; but he had no equal in the sewing part of the business. Indeed, everybody knows that sailors have a remarkable aptitude for tailoring.

The cloth of which the balloon-case was made was then cleaned by means of soda and potash, obtained by the incineration of plants, in such a way that the cotton, having got rid of the varnish, resumed its natural softness and elasticity; then, exposed to the action of the atmosphere, it soon became perfectly white. Some dozen shirts and socks—the latter not knitted of course, but made of cotton—were thus manufactured. What a comfort it was to the settlers to clothe themselves again in clean linen, which was doubtless rather rough, but they were not troubled about that! and then to go to sleep between sheets, which made the couches at Granite House into quite comfortable beds!

It was about this time also that they made boots of seal-leather, which were greatly needed to replace the shoes and boots brought from America. We may be sure that these new shoes were large enough and never pinched the feet of the wearers.

With the beginning of the year 1866 the heat was very great, but the hunting in the forests did not stand still. Agoutis, peccaries, capybaras, kangaroos, game of all sorts, actually swarmed there, and Spilett and Herbert were too good marksmen ever to throw away their shot uselessly.

Cyrus Harding still recommended them to husband the ammunition, and he took measures to replace the powder and shot which had been found in the box, and which he wished to reserve

57

for the future. How did he know where chance might one day cast his companions and himself in the event of their leaving their domain? They should, then, prepare for the unknown future by husbanding their ammunition and by substituting for it some easily renewable substance.

To replace lead, of which Harding had found no traces in the island, he employed granulated iron, which was easy to manufacture. These bullets, not having the weight of leaden bullets, were made larger, and each charge contained less, but the skill of the sportsmen made up this deficiency. As to powder, Cyrus Harding would have been able to make that also, for he had at his disposal saltpetre, sulphur, and coal; but this preparation requires extreme care, and without special tools it is difficult to produce it of a good quality. Harding preferred, therefore, to manufacture pyroxyle, that is to say gun-cotton, a substance in which cotton is not indispensable, as the elementary tissue of vegetables may be used, and this is found in an almost pure state, not only in cotton, but in the textile fibres of hemp and flax, in paper, the pith of the elder, etc. Now, the elder abounded in the island towards the mouth of Red Creek, and the colonists had already made coffee of the berries of these shrubs, which belong to the family of the caprifoliaceæ.

The only thing to be collected, therefore, was elder-pith, for as to the other substance necessary for the manufacture of pyroxyle, it was only fuming azotic acid. Now, Harding having sulphuric acid at his disposal, had already been easily able to produce azotic acid by attacking the saltpetre with which nature supplied him. He accordingly resolved to manufacture and employ pyroxyle, although it has some inconveniences, that is to say, a great inequality of effect, an excessive inflammability, since it takes fire at one hundred and seventy degrees instead of two hundred and forty, and lastly, an instantaneous deflagration which might damage the firearms. On the other hand, the advantages of pyroxyle consist in this, that it is not injured by damp, that it does not make the gun-barrels dirty, and that its force is four times that of ordinary powder.

To make pyroxyle, the cotton must be immersed in the fuming azotic acid for a quarter of an hour, then washed in cold water and dried. Nothing could be more simple.

Cyrus Harding had only at his disposal the ordinary azotic acid and not the fuming or monohydrate azotic acid, that is to say, acid which emits white vapours when it comes in contact with damp air; but by substituting for the latter ordinary azotic acid, mixed, in the proportion of from three to five volumes of concentrated sulphuric acid, the engineer obtained the same result. The sportsmen of the island therefore soon had a perfectly prepared substance, which, employed discreetly, produced admirable results.

About this time the settlers cleared three acres of the plateau, and the rest was preserved in a wild state, for the benefit of the onagas. Several excursions were made into the Jacamar woods and forests of the Far West, and they brought back from thence a large collection of wild vegetables, spinage, cress, radishes, and turnips, which careful culture would soon improve, and which would temper the regimen on which the settlers had till then subsisted. Supplies of wood and coal were also carted. Each excursion was at the same time a means of improving the roads, which gradually became smoother under the wheels of the cart.

The rabbit-warren still continued to supply the larder of Granite House. As fortunately it was situated on the other side of Creek Glycerine, its inhabitants could not reach the plateau nor ravage the newly-made plantation. The oyster-bed among the rocks was frequently renewed, and furnished excellent molluscs. Besides that, the fishing, either in the lake or the Mercy, was very profitable, for Pencroft had made some lines, armed with iron hooks, with which they frequently caught fine trout, and a species of fish whose silvery sides were speckled with yellow, and which were also extremely savoury. Master Neb, who was skilled in the culinary art, knew how to vary agreeably the bill of fare. Bread alone was wanting at the table of the settlers, and as has been said, they felt this privation greatly.

The settlers hunted too the turtles which frequented the shores of Cape Mandible. At this place the beach was covered with little mounds, concealing perfectly spherical turtles' eggs, with white hard shells, the albumen of which does not coagulate as that of birds' eggs. They were hatched by the sun, and their number was naturally considerable, as each turtle can lay annually two hundred and fifty.

"A regular egg-field," observed Gideon Spilett, "and we have nothing to do but to pick them up."

But not being contented with simply the produce, they made chase after the producers, the result of which was that they were able to bring back to Granite House a dozen of these chelonians, which were really valuable in an alimentary point of view. The turtle soup, flavoured with aromatic herbs, often gained well-merited praises for its preparer, Neb.

We must here mention another fortunate circumstance by which new stores for the winter were laid in. Shoals of salmon entered the Mercy, and ascended the country for several miles. It was the time at which the females, going to find suitable places in which to spawn, precede the males and make a great noise through the fresh water. A thousand of these fish, which measured about two feet and a half in length, came up the river, and a large quantity were retained by fixing dams across the stream. More than a hundred were thus taken, which were salted and stored for the time when winter, freezing up the streams, would render fishing impracticable. By this time the intelligent Jup was raised to the duty of valet. He had been dressed in a jacket, white linen breeches, and an apron, the pockets of which were his delight. The clever orang had been marvellously trained by Neb, and any one would have said that the negro and the ape understood each other when they talked together. Jup had besides a real affection for Neb, and Neb returned it. When his services were not required, either for carrying wood or for climbing to the top of some tree, Jup passed the greatest part of his time in the kitchen, where he endeavoured to imitate Neb in all that he saw him do. The black showed the greatest patience and even extreme zeal in instructing his pupil, and the pupil exhibited remarkable intelligence in profiting by the lessons he received from his master.

Judge then of the pleasure Master Jup gave to the inhabitants of Granite House when, without their having had any idea of it, he appeared one day, napkin on his arm, ready to wait at table. Quick, attentive, he acquitted himself perfectly, changing the plates, bringing dishes, pouring out water, all with a gravity which gave intense amusement to the settlers, and which enraptured Pencroft.

"Jup, some soup!"

"Jup, a little agouti!"

"Jup, a plate!"

"Jup! Good Jup! Honest Jup!"

Nothing was heard but that, and Jup without ever being disconcerted, replied to every one, watched for everything, and he shook his head in a knowing way when Pencroft, referring to his joke of the first day, said to him,—

"Decidedly, Jup, your wages must be doubled."

It is useless to say that the orang was now thoroughly domesticated at Granite House, and that he often accompanied his masters to the forest without showing any wish to leave them. It was most amusing to see him walking with a stick which Pencroft had given him, and which he carried on his shoulder like a gun. If they wished to gather some fruit from the summit of a tree, how quickly he climbed for it! If the wheel of the cart, stuck in the mud, with what energy did Jup with a single heave of his shoulder put it right again.

"What a jolly fellow he is!" cried Pencroft often. "If he was as mischievous as he is good, there would be no doing any thing with him!"

It was towards the end of January the colonists began their labours in the centre of the island. It had been decided that a corral should be established near the sources of the Red Creek, at the foot of Mount Franklin, destined to contain the ruminants, whose presence would have been troublesome at Granite House, and especially for the musmons, who were to supply the wool for the settlers' winter garments.

Each morning, the colony, sometimes entire, but more often represented only by Harding, Herbert, and Pencroft, proceeded to the sources of the Creek, a distance of not more than five miles, by the newly beaten road to which the name of Corral Road had been given.

There a site was chosen, at the back of the southern ridge of the mountain. It was a meadow land, dotted here and there with clumps of trees, and watered by a little stream, which sprung from the slopes which closed it in on one side. The grass was fresh, and it was not too much shaded by the trees which grew about it. This meadow was to be surrounded by a palisade, high enough to prevent even the most agile animals from leaping over. This enclosure would be large enough to contain a hundred musmons and wild goats, with all the young ones they might produce.

The perimeter of the corral was then traced by the engineer, and they would then have proceeded to fell the trees necessary for the construction of the palisade, but as the opening up of the road had already necessitated the sacrifice of a considerable number, those were brought and supplied a hundred stakes, which were firmly fixed in the ground.

At the front of the palisade a large entrance was reserved, and closed with strong folding-doors.

The construction of this corral did not take less than three weeks, for besides the palisade, Cyrus Harding built large sheds, in which the animals could take shelter. These buildings had also to be made very strong, for musmons are powerful animals, and their first fury was to be feared. The stakes, sharpened at their upper end and hardened by fire, had been fixed by means of cross-bars, and at regular distances props assured the solidity of the whole.

The corral finished, a raid had to be made on the pastures

frequented by the ruminants. This was done on the 7th of February, on a beautiful summer's day, and every one took part in it. The onagas, already well trained, were ridden by Spilett and Herbert, and were of great use.

The manœuvre consisted simply in surrounding the musmons and goats, and gradually narrowing the circle around them. Cyrus Harding, Pencroft, Neb, and Jup, posted themselves in different parts of the wood, whilst the two cavaliers and Top galloped in a radius of half a mile round the corral.

The musmons were very numerous in this part of the island. These fine animals were as large as deer; their horns were stronger than those of the ram, and their grey-coloured fleece was mixed with long hair.

This hunting day was very fatiguing. Such going and coming, and running and riding and shouting! Of a hundred musmons which had been surrounded, more than two-thirds escaped, but at last, thirty of these animals and ten wild goats were gradually driven back towards the corral, the open door of which appearing to offer a means of escape, they rushed in and were prisoners.

In short, the result was satisfactory, and the settlers had no reason to complain. There was no doubt that the flock would prosper, and that at no distant time not only wool but hides would be abundant.

That evening the hunters returned to Granite House quite exhausted. However, notwithstanding their fatigue, they returned the next day to visit the corral. The prisoners had been trying to overthrow the palisade, but of course had not succeeded, and were not long in becoming more tranquil.

During the month of February, no event of any importance occurred. The daily labours were pursued methodically, and, as well as improving the roads to the corral and to Port Balloon, a third was commenced, which, starting from the enclosure, proceeded towards the western coast. The yet unknown portion of Lincoln Island was that of the wood-covered Serpentine Peninsula, which sheltered the wild beasts, from which Gideon Spilett was so anxious to clear their domain.

Before the cold season should appear the most assiduous care was given to the cultivation of the wild plants which had been transplanted from the forest to Prospect Heights. Herbert never returned from an excursion without bringing home some useful vegetable. One day, it was some specimens of the chicory tribe, the seeds of which by pressure yield an excellent oil; another, it was some common sorrel, whose anti-scorbutic qualities were not to be despised; then, some of those precious tubers, which have at all times been cultivated in South America, potatoes, of which more than two hundred species are now known. The kitchen garden, now well stocked and carefully defended from the birds, was divided into small beds, where grew lettuces, kidney potatoes, sorrel, turnips, radishes, and other cruciferæ. The soil on the plateau was particularly fertile, and it was hoped that the harvests would be abundant.

They had also a variety of different beverages, and so long as they did not demand wine, the most hard to please would have had no reason to complain. To the Oswego tea, and the fermented liquor extracted from the roots of the dragonnier, Harding had added a regular beer, made from the young shoots of the spruce-fir, which, after having been boiled and fermented, made that agreeable drink, called by the Anglo-Americans spring-beer.

Towards the end of the summer, the poultry-yard was possessed of a couple of fine bustards, which belonged to the houbara species, characterised by a sort of feathery mantle; a dozen shovellers, whose upper mandible was prolonged on each side by a membraneous appendage; and also some magnificent cocks, similar to the Mozambique cocks, the comb, caruncle and epidermis being black. So far, everything had succeeded, thanks to the activity of these courageous and intelligent men. Nature did much for them, doubtless; but faithful to the great precept, they made a right use of what a bountiful Providence gave them.

After the heat of these warm summer days, in the evening when their work was finished and the sea breeze began to blow, they liked to sit on the edge of Prospect Heights, in a sort of verandah, covered with creepers, which Neb had made with his own hands. There they talked, they instructed each other, they made plans, and the rough good-humour of the sailor always amused this little world, in which the most perfect harmony had never ceased to reign.

They often spoke of their country, of their dear and great America. What was the result of the War of Secession? It could not have been greatly prolonged, Richmond had doubtless soon fallen into the hands of General Grant. The taking of the capital of the Confederates must have been the last action of this terrible struggle. Now the North had triumphed in the good cause, how welcome would have been a newspaper to the exiles in Lincoln Island! For eleven months all communication between them and the rest of their fellow-creatures had been interrupted, and in a short time the 24th of March would arrive, the anniversary of the day on which the balloon had thrown them on this unknown coast. They were then mere castaways, not even knowing how they should preserve their miserable lives from the fury of the elements! And now, thanks to the knowledge of their captain, and their own intelligence, they were regular colonists, furnished with arms, tools, and instruments; they had been able to turn to their profit the animals, plants, and minerals of the island, that is to say, the three kingdoms of Nature.

Yes; they often talked of all these things and formed still more plans for the future.

As to Cyrus Harding he was for the most part silent, and listened to his companions more often than he spoke to them. Sometimes he smiled at Herbert's ideas or Pencroft's nonsense, but always and everywhere he pondered over those inexplicable facts, that strange enigma, of which the secret still escaped him!

CHAPTER IX

Bad Weather—The Hydraulic Lift—Manufacture of Glass-ware—The Bread-tree—Frequent Visits to the Corral—Increase of the Flock—The Reporter's Question—Exact Position of Lincoln Island—Pencroft's Proposal.

The weather changed during the first week of March. There had been a full moon at the commencement of the month, and the heat was still excessive. The atmosphere was felt to be full of electricity, and a period of some length of tempestuous weather was to be feared.

Indeed, on the 2nd, peals of thunder were heard, the wind blew from the east, and hail rattled against the façade of Granite House like volleys of grape-shot. The door and windows were immediately closed, or everything in the rooms would have been drenched. On seeing these hailstones, some of which were the size of a pigeon's egg, Pencroft's first thought was that his cornfield was in serious danger.

He directly rushed to his field, where little green heads were already appearing, and, by means of a great cloth, he managed to protect his crop.

This bad weather lasted a week, during which time the thunder rolled without cessation in the depths of the sky.

The colonists, not having any pressing work out of doors, profited by the bad weather to work at the interior of Granite House, the arrangement of which was becoming more complete from day to day. The engineer made a turning-lathe, with which he turned several articles both for the toilet and the kitchen, particularly buttons, the want of which was greatly felt. A gun-rack had been made for the firearms, which were kept with extreme care, and neither tables nor cupboards were left incomplete. They sawed, they planed, they filed, they turned: and during the whole of this bad season, nothing was heard but the grinding of tools or the humming of the turning-lathe which responded to the growling of the thunder.

Master Jup had not been forgotten, and he occupied a room at the back, near the storeroom, a sort of cabin with a cot always full of good litter, which perfectly suited his taste.

"With good old Jup there is never any quarrelling," often repeated Pencroft, "never any improper reply! What a servant, Neb, what a servant!"

Of course Jup was now well used to service. He brushed their clothes, he turned the spit, he waited at table, he swept the rooms, he gathered wood, and he performed another admirable piece of service which delighted Pencroft—he never went to sleep without first coming to tuck up the worthy sailor in his bed.

As to the health of the members of the colony, bipeds or bimana, quadrumana or quadrupeds, it left nothing to be desired. With their life in the open air, on this salubrious soil, under that temperate zone, working both with head and hands, they could not suppose that illness would ever attack them.

All were indeed wonderfully well. Herbert had already grown two inches in the year. His figure was forming and becoming more manly, and he promised to be an accomplished man, physically as well as morally. Besides, he improved himself during the leisure hours which manual occupations left to him; he read the books found in the case; and after the practical lessons which were taught by the very necessity of their position, he found in the engineer for science, and the reporter for languages, masters who were delighted to complete his education.

The tempest ended about the 9th of March, but the sky remained covered with clouds during the whole of this last summer month. The atmosphere, violently agitated by the electric commotions, could not recover its former purity, and there was almost invariably rain and fog, except for three or four fine days on which several excursions were made. About this time the female onaga gave birth to a young one which belonged to the same sex as its mother, and which throve capitally. In the corral, the flock of musmons had also increased, and several lambs already bleated in the sheds, to the great delight of Neb and Herbert, who had each their favourite among these new-comers. An attempt was also made for the domestication of the peccaries, which succeeded well. A sty was constructed near the poultry-yard, and soon contained several young ones in the way to become civilised, that is to say, to become fat under Neb's care. Master Jup, entrusted with carrying them their daily nourishment, leavings from the kitchen, etc., acquitted himself conscientiously of his task. He sometimes amused himself at the expense of his little pensioners by tweaking their tails; but this was mischief, and not wickedness, for these little twisted tails amused him like a plaything, and his instinct was that of a child. One day in this month of March, Pencroft, talking to the engineer, reminded Cyrus Harding of a promise which the latter had not as yet had time to fulfil.

"You once spoke of an apparatus which would take the place

of the long ladders at Granite House, captain," said he; "won't you make it some day?"

"Nothing will be easier; but is this a really useful thing?"

"Certainly, captain. After we have given ourselves necessaries, let us think a little of luxury. For us it may be luxury, if you like, but for things it is necessary. It isn't very convenient to climb up a long ladder when one is heavily loaded."

"Well, Pencroft, we will try to please you," replied Cyrus Harding.

"But you have no machine at your disposal."

"We will make one."

"A steam machine?"

"No, a water machine."

And, indeed, to work his apparatus there was already a natural force at the disposal of the engineer which could be used without great difficulty. For this, it was enough to augment the flow of the little stream which supplied the interior of Granite House with water. The opening among the stones and grass was then increased, thus producing a strong fall at the bottom of the passage, the overflow from which escaped by the inner well. Below this fall the engineer fixed a cylinder with paddles, which was joined on the exterior with a strong cable rolled on a wheel, supporting a basket. In this way, by means of a long rope reaching to the ground, which enabled them to regulate the motive power, they could rise in the basket to the door of Granite House.

It was on the 17th of March that the lift acted for the first time, and gave universal satisfaction. Henceforward all the loads, wood, coal, provisions, and even the settlers themselves, were hoisted by this simple system, which replaced the primitive ladder, and, as may be supposed, no one thought of regretting the change. Top particularly was enchanted with this improvement, for he had not, and never could have possessed Master Jup's skill in climbing ladders, and often it was on Neb's back, or even on that of the orang, that he had been obliged to make the ascent to Granite House. About this time, too, Cyrus Harding attempted to manufacture glass and he at first put the old pottery-kiln to this new use. There were some difficulties to be encountered, but after several fruitless attempts, he succeeded in setting up a glass manufactory, which Gideon Spilett and Herbert, his usual assistants did not leave for several days. As to the substances used in the composition of glass, they are simply sand, chalk and soda, either carbonate or sulphate. Now the beach supplied sand, lime supplied chalk, sea weeds supplied soda, pyrites supplied sulphuric acid and the ground supplied coal to heat the kiln to the wished-for temperature. Cyrus Harding thus soon had every thing ready for setting to work.

The tool, the manufacture of which presented the most difficulty, was the pipe of the glass maker, an iron tube, five or six feet long, which collects on one end the material in a state of fusion. But by means of a long, thin piece of iron rolled up like the barrel of a gun, Pencroft succeeded in making a tube soon ready for use.

On the 28th of March the tube was heated. A hundred parts of sand thirty-five of chalk, forty of sulphate of soda, mixed with two or three parts of powered coal, composed the substance which was placed in crucibles. When the high temperature of the oven had reduced it to a liquid, or rather a pasty state, Cyrus Harding collected with the tube a quantity of the paste, he turned it about on a metal plate previously arranged so as to give it a form suitable for blowing, then he passed the tube to Herbert, telling him to blow at the other extremity.

And Herbert, swelling out his cheeks, blew so much and so well into the tube—taking care to twirl it round at the same time—that his breath dilated the glassy mass. Other quantities of the substance in a state of fusion were added to the first, and in a short time the result was a bubble which measured a foot in diameter. Harding then took the tube out of Herbert's hands, and, giving to it a pendulous motion, he ended by lengthening the malleable bubble so as to give it a cylindro-conic shape.

The blowing operation had given a cylinder of glass terminated by two hemispheric caps, which were easily detached by means of a sharp iron dipped in cold water; then, by the same proceeding, this cylinder was cut lengthways, and after having been rendered malleable by a second heating, it was extended on a plate and spread out with a wooden roller.

The first pane was thus manufactured, and they had only to perform this operation fifty times to have fifty panes. The windows at Granite House were soon furnished with panes; not very white, perhaps, but still sufficiently transparent.

As to bottles and tumblers, that was only play. They were satisfied with them, besides, just as they came from the end of the tube. Pencroft had asked to be allowed to "blow" in his turn, and it was great fun for him; but he blew so hard that his productions took the most ridiculous shapes, which he admired immensely.

Cyrus Harding and Herbert, whilst hunting one day, had entered the forest of the Far West, on the left bank of the Mercy, and, as usual, the lad was asking a thousand questions of the engineer, who answered them heartily. Now, as Harding was not a sportsman, and as, on the other side, Herbert was talking chemistry and natural philosophy, numbers of kangaroos, capybaras, and agoutis came within range, which, however, escaped the lad's gun; the consequence was that the day was already advanced, and the two hunters were in danger of having made a useless excursion, when Herbert, stopping, and uttering a cry of joy, exclaimed,—

"Oh, Captain Harding, do you see that tree?" and he pointed to a shrub, rather than a tree, for it was composed of a single stem, covered with a scaly bark, which bore leaves streaked with little parallel veins.

"And what is this tree which resembles a little palm?" asked Harding.

"It is a 'cycas revoluta,' of which I have a picture in our dictionary of Natural History!" said Herbert.

"But I can't see any fruit on this shrub!" observed his companion.

"No, captain," replied Herbert; "but its stem contains a flour with which nature has provided us all ready ground."

"It is, then, the bread-tree?"

"Yes, the bread-tree."

"Well, my boy," replied the engineer, "this is a valuable discovery, since our wheat harvest is not yet ripe; I hope that you are not mistaken!"

Herbert was not mistaken: he broke the stem of a cycas, which was composed of a glandulous tissue, containing a quantity of floury pith, traversed with woody fibre, separated by rings of the same substance, arranged concentrically. With this fecula was mingled a mucilaginous juice of disagreeable flavour, but which it would be easy to get rid of by pressure. This cellular substance was regular flour of a superior quality, extremely nourishing; its exportation was formerly forbidden by the Japanese laws.

Cyrus Harding and Herbert, after having examined that part of the Far West where the cycas grew, took their bearings, and returned to Granite House, where they made known their discovery.

The next day the settlers went to collect some and returned to Granite House with an ample supply of cycas stems. The engineer constructed a press, with which to extract the mucilaginous juice mingled with the fecula, and he obtained a large quantity of flour, which Neb soon transformed into cakes and puddings. This was not quite real wheaten bread, but it was very like it.

Now, too, the onaga, the goats, and the sheep in the corral furnished daily the milk necessary to the colony. The cart, or rather a sort of light carriole which had replaced it, made frequent journeys to the corral, and when it was Pencroft's turn to go he took Jup, and let him drive, and Jup, cracking his whip, acquitted himself with his customary intelligence.

Everything prospered, as well in the corral as in Granite House and certainly the settlers, if it had not been that they were so far from their native land, had no reason to complain. They were so well suited to this life, and were, besides, so accustomed to the island, that they could not have left its hospitable soil without regret!

And yet so deeply is the love of his country implanted in the heart of man, that if a ship had unexpectedly come in sight of the island, the colonists would have made signals, would have attracted her attention, and would have departed!

It was the 1st of April, a Sunday, Easter Day, which Harding and his companions sanctified by rest and prayer. The day was fine, such as an October day in the northern hemisphere might be.

All, towards the evening after dinner, were seated under the verandah on the edge of Prospect Heights, and they were watching the darkness creeping up from the horizon. Some cups of the infusion of elder berries, which took the place of coffee, had been served by Neb. They were speaking of the island and of its isolated situation in the Pacific, which led Gideon Spilett to say,—

"My dear Cyrus, have you ever, since you possessed the sextant found in the case, again taken the position of our island?"

"No," replied the engineer

"But it would perhaps be a good thing to do it with this instrument, which is more perfect than that which you before used."

"What is the good?" said Pencroft. "The island is quite comfortable where it is!"

"Well, who knows," returned the reporter, "who knows but that we may be much nearer inhabited land than we think?"

"We shall know to morrow," replied Cyrus Harding, "and if it had not been for the occupations which left me no leisure, we should have known it already."

"Good!" said Pencroft. "The captain is too good an observer to be mistaken, and, if it has not moved from its place, the island is just where he put it."

"We shall see."

On the next day, therefore, by means of the sextant, the engineer made the necessary observations to verify the position which he had already obtained, and this was the result of his operation. His first observation had given him for the situation of Lincoln Island,—

In west longitude: from 150° to 155°;
In south latitude: from 30° to 35°.

The second gave exactly:

In longitude: 150° 30′;
In south latitude: 34° 57′.

So then, notwithstanding the imperfection of his apparatus, Cyrus Harding had operated with so much skill that his error did not exceed five degrees.

"Now," said Gideon Spilett, "since we possess an atlas as well as a sextant, let us see, my dear Cyrus, the exact position which Lincoln Island occupies in the Pacific."

Herbert fetched the atlas, and the map of the Pacific was opened, and the engineer, compass in hand, prepared to determine their position.

Suddenly the compasses stopped, and he exclaimed,—

"But an island exists in this part of the Pacific already!"

"An island?" cried Pencroft.

"Tabor Island."

"An important island?"

"No, an islet lost in the Pacific, and which perhaps has never been visited."

"Well, we will visit it," said Pencroft.

"We?"

"Yes, captain. We will build a decked boat, and I will undertake to steer her. At what distance are we from this Tabor Island?"

"About a hundred and fifty miles to the north-east," replied Harding.

"A hundred and fifty miles! And what's that?" returned Pencroft. "In forty-eight hours, with a good wind, we should sight it!"

And, on this reply, it was decided that a vessel should be constructed in time to be launched towards the month of next October, on the return of the fine season.

CHAPTER X

Boat-building—Second Crop of Corn—Hunting Koalas—A new Plant, more Pleasant than Useful—Whale in Sight—A Harpoon from the Vineyard—Cutting up the Whale—Use for the Bones—End of the Month of May—Pencroft has nothing left to wish for.

When Pencroft had once got a plan into his head, he had no peace till it was executed. Now he wished to visit Tabor Island, and as a boat of a certain size was necessary for this voyage, he determined to build one.

What wood should be employed? Elm or fir, both of which abounded in the island? They decided for the fir, as being easy to work, but which stands water as well as the elm.

These details settled, it was agreed that since the fine season would not return before six months, Cyrus Harding and Pencroft should work alone at the boat. Gideon Spilett and Herbert were to continue to hunt, and neither Neb nor Master Jup his assistant were to leave the domestic duties which had devolved upon them.

Directly the trees were chosen, they were felled, stripped of their branches, and sawn into planks as well as sawyers would have been able to do it. A week after, in the recess between the Chimneys and the cliff, a dockyard was prepared, and a keel five-and-thirty feet long, furnished with a stern-post at the stern and a stem at the bows, lay along the sand.

Cyrus Harding was not working in the dark at this new trade. He knew as much about ship-building as about nearly everything else, and he had at first drawn the model of his ship on paper. Besides, he was ably seconded by Pencroft, who, having worked for several years in a dockyard at Brooklyn, knew the practical part of the trade. It was not until after careful calculation and deep thought that the timbers were laid on the keel.

Pencroft, as may be believed, was all eagerness to carry out his new enterprise, and would not leave his work for an instant.

A single thing had the honour of drawing him, but for one day only, from his dockyard. This was the second wheat-harvest, which was gathered in on the 15th of April. It was as much a success as the first, and yielded the number of grains which had been predicted.

"Five bushels, captain," said Pencroft, after having scrupulously measured his treasure.

"Five bushels," replied the engineer; "and a hundred and

72

thirty thousand grains a bushel will make six hundred and fifty thousand grains."

"Well, we will sow them all this time," said the sailor, "except a little in reserve."

"Yes, Pencroft, and if the next crop gives a proportionate yield, we shall have four thousand bushels."

"And shall we eat bread?"

"We shall eat bread."

"But we must have a mill."

"We will make one."

The third cornfield was very much larger than the two first, and the soil, prepared with extreme care, received the precious seed. That done, Pencroft returned to his work.

During this time Spilett and Herbert hunted in the neighbourhood, and they ventured deep into the still unknown parts of the Far West, their guns loaded with ball, ready for any dangerous emergency. It was a vast thicket of magnificent trees, crowded together as if pressed for room. The exploration of these dense masses of wood was difficult in the extreme, and the reporter never ventured there without the pocket-compass, for the sun scarcely pierced through the thick foliage, and it would have been very difficult for them to retrace their way. It naturally happened that game was more rare in those situations where there was hardly sufficient room to move; two or three large herbivorous animals were however killed during the last fortnight of April. These were koalas, specimens of which the settlers had already seen to the north of the lake, and which stupidly allowed themselves to be killed among the thick branches of the trees in which they took refuge. Their skins were brought back to Granite House, and there, by the help of sulphuric acid, they were subjected to a sort of tanning process which rendered them capable of being used.

On the 30th of April, the two sportsmen were in the depth of the Far West, when the reporter, preceding Herbert a few paces, arrived in a sort of clearing, into which the trees more sparsely scattered had permitted a few rays to penetrate. Gideon Spilett was at first surprised at the odour which exhaled from certain plants with straight stalks, round and branchy, bearing grape-like clusters of flowers and very small berries. The reporter broke off one or two of these stalks and returned to the lad, to whom he said,—

"What can this be, Herbert?"

"Well, Mr. Spilett," said Herbert, "this is a treasure which will secure you Pencroft's gratitude for ever."

"Is it tobacco?"

"Yes, and though it may not be of the first quality, it is none the less tobacco!"

"Oh, good old Pencroft! Won't he be pleased? But we must not let him smoke it all, he must give us our share."

"Ah! an idea occurs to me, Mr. Spilett," replied Herbert. "Don't let us say anything to Pencroft yet; we will prepare these leaves, and one fine day we will present him with a pipe already filled!"

"All right, Herbert, and on that day our worthy companion will have nothing left to wish for in this world."

The reporter and the lad secured a good store of the precious plant, and then returned to Granite House, where they smuggled it in with as much precaution as if Pencroft had been the most vigilant and severe of custom-house officers.

Cyrus Harding and Neb were taken into confidence, and the sailor suspected nothing during the whole time, necessarily somewhat long, which was required in order to dry the small leaves, chop them up, and subject them to a certain torrefaction on hot stones. This took two months; but all these manipulations were successfully carried on unknown to Pencroft, for, occupied with the construction of his boat, he only returned to Granite House at the hour of rest.

For some days they had observed an enormous animal two or three miles out in the open sea swimming around Lincoln Island. This was a whale of the largest size, which apparently belonged to the southern species, called the "Cape Whale."

"What a lucky chance it would be if we could capture it!" cried the sailor. "Ah, if we only had a proper boat and a good harpoon, I would say, 'After the beast,' for he would be well worth the trouble of catching!"

"Well, Pencroft," observed Harding, "I should much like to watch you handling a harpoon. It would be very interesting."

"I am astonished," said the reporter, "to see a whale in this comparatively high latitude."

"Why so, Mr. Spilett?" replied Herbert. "We are exactly in that part of the Pacific which English and American whalemen call the whale field, and it is here, between New Zealand and South America, that the whales of the southern hemisphere are met with in the greatest numbers."

And Pencroft returned to his work, not without uttering a sigh of regret, for every sailor is a born fisherman, and if the pleasure of fishing is in exact proportion to the size of the animal, one can judge how a whaler feels in sight of a whale. And if this had only been for pleasure! But they could not help feeling how valuable such a prize would have been to the colony, for the oil, the fat, and the bones would have been put to many uses.

Now it happened that this whale appeared to have no wish to leave the waters of the island. Therefore, whether from the windows of Granite House, or from Prospect Heights, Herbert and Gideon Spilett, when they were not hunting, or Neb unless presiding over his fires, never left the telescope, but watched all the animal's movements. The cetacean, having entered far into Union Bay, made rapid furrows across it from Mandible Cape to Claw Cape, propelled by its enormously powerful flukes, on which it supported itself, and making its way through the water at the rate little short of twelve knots an hour. Sometimes also it approached so near to the island that it could be clearly distinguished. It was the southern whale, which is completely black, the head being more depressed than that of the northern whale.

They could also see it throwing up from its air-holes to a great height, a cloud of vapour, or of water, for, strange as it may appear, naturalists and whalers are not agreed on this subject. Is it air or is it water which is thus driven out? It is generally admitted to be vapour, which, condensing suddenly by contact with the cold air, falls again as rain.

However, the presence of this mammifer preoccupied the colonists. It irritated Pencroft especially as he could think of nothing else while at work. He ended by longing for it, like a child for a thing which it has been denied. At night he talked about it in his sleep, and certainly if he had had the means of attacking it, if the sloop had been in a fit state to put to sea, he would not have hesitated to set out in pursuit.

But what the colonists could not do for themselves, chance did for them, and on the 3rd of May, shouts from Neb, who had stationed himself at the kitchen window, announced that the whale was stranded on the beach of the island.

Herbert and Gideon Spilett, who were just about to set out hunting, left their guns, Pencroft threw down his axe, and Harding and Neb joining their companions, all rushed towards the scene of action.

The stranding had taken place on the beach of Flotsam Point, three miles from Granite House, and at high tide. It was therefore probable that the cetacean would not be able to extricate itself easily, at any rate it was best to hasten, so as to cut off its retreat if necessary. They ran with pick-axes and iron-tipped poles in their hands, passed over the Mercy bridge, descended the right bank of

75

the river, along the beach, and in less than twenty minutes the settlers were close to the enormous animal, above which flocks of birds already hovered.

"What a monster!" cried Neb.

And the exclamation was natural, for it was a southern whale, eighty feet long, a giant of the species, probably not weighing less than a hundred and fifty thousand pounds!

In the meanwhile, the monster thus stranded did not move, nor attempt by struggling to regain the water whilst the tide was still high.

It was dead, and a harpoon was sticking out of its left side.

"There are whalers in these quarters, then?" said Gideon Spilett directly.

"Oh, Mr Spilett, that doesn't prove anything!" replied Pencroft. "Whales have been known to go thousands of miles with a harpoon in the side, and this one might even have been struck in the north of the Atlantic and come to die in the south of the Pacific, and it would be nothing astonishing."

Pencroft, having torn the harpoon from the animal's side, read this inscription on it:—

"'MARIA   STELLA,'
"VINEYARD."

"A vessel from the Vineyard! A ship from my country!" he cried. "The *Maria Stella*! A fine whaler, 'pon my word; I know her well! Oh, my friends, a vessel from the Vineyard!—a whaler from the Vineyard!"[1]

And the sailor brandishing the harpoon, repeated, not without emotion, the name which he loved so well—the name of his birthplace.

But as it could not be expected that the *Maria Stella* would come to reclaim the animal harpooned by her, they resolved to begin cutting it up before decomposition should commence. The birds, who had watched this rich prey for several days, had determined to take possession of it without further delay, and it was necessary to drive them off by firing at them repeatedly.

The whale was a female, and a large quantity of milk was taken from it, which, according to the opinion of the naturalist Duffenbach, might pass for cow's milk, and, indeed, it differs from it neither in taste, colour, nor density.

Pencroft had formerly served on board a whaling-ship, and he could methodically direct the operation of cutting up—a sufficiently

---

[1] A port in the State of New York.

disagreeable operation lasting three days, but from which the settlers did not flinch, not even Gideon Spilett, who, as the sailor said, would end by making a "real good castaway."

The blubber, cut in parallel slices of two feet and a half in thickness, then divided into pieces which might weigh about a thousand pounds each, was melted down in large earthen pots brought to the spot, for they did not wish to taint the environs of Granite House, and in this fusion it lost nearly a third of its weight.

But there was an immense quantity of it; the tongue alone yielded six thousand pounds of oil, and the lower lip four thousand. Then, besides the fat, which would insure for a long time a store of stearine and glycerine, there were still the bones, for which a use could doubtless be found, although there were neither umbrellas nor stays used at Granite House. The upper part of the mouth of the cetacean was, indeed, provided on both sides with eight hundred horny blades, very elastic, of a fibrous texture, and fringed at the edge like great combs, of which the teeth, six feet long, served to retain the thousands of animalculæ, little fish, and molluscs, on which the whale fed.

The operation finished, to the great satisfaction of the operators, the remains of the animal were left to the birds, who would soon make every vestige of it disappear, and their usual daily occupations were resumed by the inmates of Granite House.

However, before returning to the dockyard, Cyrus Harding conceived the idea of fabricating certain machines, which greatly excited the curiosity of his companions. He took a dozen of the whale's bones, cut them into six equal parts, and sharpened their ends.

"This machine is not my own invention, and it is frequently employed by the Aleutian hunters in Russian America. You see these bones, my friends; well, when it freezes, I will bend them, and then wet them with water till they are entirely covered with ice, which will keep them bent, and I will strew them on the snow, having previously covered them with fat. Now, what will happen if a hungry animal swallows one of these baits? Why, the heat of his stomach will melt the ice, and the bone, springing straight, will pierce him with its sharp points."

"Well! I do call that ingenious!" said Pencroft.

"And it will spare the powder and shot," rejoined Cyrus Harding.

"That will be better than traps!" added Neb.

In the meanwhile the boat-building progressed, and towards the end of the month half the planking was completed. It could already be seen that her shape was excellent, and that she would sail well.

Pencroft worked with unparalleled ardour, and only a sturdy frame could have borne such fatigue; but his companions were preparing in secret a reward for his labours, and on the 31st of May he was to meet with one of the greatest joy's of his life.

On that day, after dinner, just as he was about to leave the table, Pencroft felt a hand on his shoulder.

It was the hand of Gideon Spilett, who said,—

"One moment, Master Pencroft, you mustn't sneak off like that! You've forgotten your dessert."

"Thank you, Mr. Spilett," replied the sailor, "I am going back to my work."

"Well a cup of coffee, my friend?"

"Nothing more."

"A pipe, then?"

Pencroft jumped up, and his great good-natured face grew pale when he saw the reporter presenting him with a ready-filled pipe, and Herbert with a glowing coal.

The sailor endeavoured to speak, but could not get out a word, so, seizing the pipe, he carried it to his lips, then applying the coal, he drew five or six great whiffs. A fragrant blue cloud soon arose, and from its depths a voice was heard repeating excitedly,—

"Tobacco! real tobacco!"

"Yes, Pencroft," returned Cyrus Harding, "and very good tobacco too!"

"O divine Providence! sacred Author of all things!" cried the sailor. "Nothing more is now wanting to our island."

And Pencroft smoked, and smoked, and smoked.

"And who made this discovery?" he asked at length. "You, Herbert, no doubt?"

"No, Pencroft, it was Mr. Spilett."

"Mr Spilett!" exclaimed the sailor seizing the reporter, and clasping him to his breast with such a squeeze that he had never felt anything like it before.

"Oh, Pencroft," said Spilett, recovering his breath at last, "a truce for one moment. You must share your gratitude with Herbert, who recognised the plant, with Cyrus, who prepared it, and with Neb who took a great deal of trouble to keep our secret."

"Well, my friends, I will repay you some day," replied the sailor. "Now we are friends for life."

CHAPTER XI

Winter—Felling Wood—The Mill—Pencroft's fixed Idea—The Bones—To what Use an Albatross may be put—Fuel for the Future—Top and Jup—Storms—Damage to the Poultry-yard—Excursion to the Marsh—Cyrus Harding alone—Exploring the Well

Winter arrived with the month of June, which is the December of the northern zones, and the great business was the making of warm and solid clothing.

The musmons in the corral had been stripped of their wool, and this precious textile material was now to be transformed into stuff.

Of course Cyrus Harding, having at his disposal neither carders, combers, polishers, stretchers, twisters, mule-jenny, nor self-acting machine to spin the wool, nor loom to weave it, was obliged to proceed in a simpler way, so as to do without spinning and weaving. And indeed he proposed to make use of the property which the filaments of wool possess when subjected to a powerful pressure of mixing together, and of manufacturing by this simple process the material called felt. This felt could then be obtained by a simple operation which, if it diminished the flexibility of the stuff, increased its power of retaining heat in proportion. Now the wool furnished by the musmons was composed of very short hairs, and was in a good condition to be felted.

The engineer, aided by his companions, including Pencroft, who was once more obliged to leave his boat, commenced the preliminary operations, the object of which was to rid the wool of that fat and oily substance with which it is impregnated, and which is called grease. This cleaning was done in vats filled with water, which was maintained at the temperature of seventy degrees, and in which the wool was soaked for four-and-twenty hours; it was then thoroughly washed in baths of soda, and, when sufficiently dried by pressure, it was in a state to be compressed, that is to say, to produce a solid material, rough, no doubt, and such as would have no value in a manufacturing centre of Europe or America, but which would be highly esteemed in the Lincoln Island markets.

This sort of material must have been known from the most ancient times, and, in fact, the first woollen stuffs were manufactured by the process which Harding was now about to employ. Where Harding's engineering qualifications now came into play was in the construction of the machine for pressing the wool, for he knew how to turn ingeniously to profit the mechanical force, hitherto unused, which the waterfall on the beach possessed to move a fulling-mill.

Nothing could be more rudimentary. The wool was placed in troughs, and upon it fell in turns heavy wooden mallets, such was the machine in question, and such it had been for centuries until the time when the mallets were replaced by cylinders of compression, and the material was no longer subjected to beating, but to regular rolling.

The operation, ably directed by Cyrus Harding, was a complete success. The wool, previously impregnated with a solution of soap, intended on the one hand to facilitate the interlacing, the compression, and the softening of the wool, and on the other to prevent its diminution by the beating, issued from the mill in the shape of thick felt cloth. The roughnesses with which the staple of wool is naturally filled were so thoroughly entangled and interlaced together that a material was formed equally suitable either for garments or bedclothes. It was certainly neither merino, muslin, cashmere, rep, satin, alpaca, cloth, nor flannel. It was "Lincolnian felt," and Lincoln Island possessed yet another manufacture. The colonists had now warm garments and thick bedclothes, and they could without fear await the approach of the winter of 1866-67.

The severe cold began to be felt about the 20th of June, and, to his great regret, Pencroft was obliged to suspend his boat-building, which he hoped to finish in time for next spring.

The sailor's great idea was to make a voyage of discovery to Tabor Island, although Harding could not approve of a voyage simply for curiosity's sake, for there was evidently nothing to be found on this desert and almost arid rock. A voyage of a hundred and fifty miles in a comparatively small vessel, over unknown seas, could not but cause him some anxiety. Suppose that their vessel, once out at sea, should be unable to reach Tabor Island, and could not return to Lincoln Island, what would become of her in the midst of the Pacific, so fruitful of disasters?

Harding often talked over this project with Pencroft, and he found him strangely bent upon undertaking this voyage, for which determination he himself could give no sufficient reason.

"Now," said the engineer one day to him, "I must observe, my friend, that after having said so much, in praise of Lincoln Island, after having spoken so often of the sorrow you would feel if you were obliged to forsake it, you are the first to wish to leave it."

"Only to leave it for a few days," replied Pencroft, "only for a few days, captain. Time to go and come back, and see what that islet is like!"

"But it is not nearly as good as Lincoln Island."

"I know that beforehand."

"Then why venture there?"

"To know what is going on in Tabor Island."

"But nothing is going on there; nothing could happen there."

"Who knows?"

"And if you are caught in a hurricane?"

"There is no fear of that in the fine season," replied Pencroft. "But, captain, as we must provide against everything, I shall ask your permission to take Herbert only with me on this voyage."

"Pencroft," replied the engineer, placing his hand on the sailor's shoulder, "if any misfortune happens to you, or to this lad, whom chance has made our child, do you think we could ever cease to blame ourselves?"

"Captain Harding," replied Pencroft, with unshaken confidence, "we shall not cause you that sorrow. Besides, we will speak further of this voyage, when the time comes to make it. And I fancy, when you have seen our tight-rigged little craft, when you have observed how she behaves at sea, when we sail round our island, for we will do so together—I fancy, I say, that you will no longer hesitate to let me go. I don't conceal from you that your boat will be a masterpiece."

"Say 'our' boat, at least, Pencroft," replied the engineer, disarmed for the moment. The conversation ended thus, to be resumed later on, without convincing either the sailor or the engineer.

The first snow fell towards the end of the month of June. The corral had previously been largely supplied with stores, so that daily visits to it were not requisite; but it was decided that more than a week should never be allowed to pass without some one going to it.

Traps were again set, and the machines manufactured by Harding were tried. The bent whalebones, imprisoned in a case of ice, and covered with a thick outer layer of fat, were placed on the border of the forest at a spot where animals usually passed on their way to the lake.

To the engineer's great satisfaction, this invention, copied from the Aleutian fishermen, succeeded perfectly. A dozen foxes, a few wild boars, and even a jaguar, were taken in this way, the animals being found dead, their stomachs pierced by the unbent bones.

81

An incident must here be related, not only as interesting in itself, but because it was the first attempt made by the colonists to communicate with the rest of mankind.

Gideon Spilett had already several times pondered whether to throw into the sea a letter enclosed in a bottle, which currents might perhaps carry to an inhabited coast, or to confide it to pigeons.

But how could it be seriously hoped that either pigeons or bottles could cross the distance of twelve hundred miles which separated the island from any inhabited land? It would have been pure folly.

But on the 30th of June the capture was effected, not without difficulty, of an albatross, which a shot from Herbert's gun had slightly wounded in the foot. It was a magnificent bird, measuring ten feet from wing to wing, and which could traverse seas as wide as the Pacific.

Herbert would have liked to keep this superb bird, as its wound would soon heal, and he thought he could tame it; but Spilett explained to him that they should not neglect this opportunity of attempting to communicate by this messenger with the lands of the Pacific; for if the albatross had come from some inhabited region, there was no doubt but that it would return there so soon as it was set free.

Perhaps in his heart Gideon Spilett, in whom the journalist sometimes came to the surface, was not sorry to have the opportunity of sending forth to take its chance an exciting article relating the adventures of the settlers in Lincoln Island. What a success for the authorised reporter of the *New York Herald*, and for the number which should contain the article, if it should ever reach the address of its editor, the Honourable John Benett!

Gideon Spilett then wrote out a concise account, which was placed in a strong waterproof bag, with an earnest request to whoever might find it to forward it to the office of the *New York Herald*. This little bag was fastened to the neck of the albatross, and not to its foot, for these birds are in the habit of resting on the surface of the sea; then liberty was given to this swift courier of the air, and it was not without some emotion that the colonists watched it disappear in the misty west.

"Where is he going to?" asked Pencroft.

"Towards New Zealand," replied Herbert.

"A good voyage to you," shouted the sailor, who himself did not expect any great result from this mode of correspondence.

With the winter, work had been resumed in the interior of Granite House, mending clothes and different occupations, amongst others making the sails for their vessel, which were cut from the inexhaustible balloon-case.

During the month of July the cold was intense, but there was no lack of either wood or coal. Cyrus Harding had established a second fireplace in the dining-room, and there the long winter evenings were spent. Talking whilst they worked, reading when the hands remained idle, the time passed with profit to all.

It was real enjoyment to the settlers when in their room, well lighted with candles, well warmed with coal, after a good dinner, elder-berry coffee smoking in the cups, the pipes giving forth an odoriferous smoke, they could hear the storm howling without. Their comfort would have been complete, if complete comfort could ever exist for those who are far from their fellow creatures, and without any means of communication with them. They often talked of their country, of the friends whom they had left, of the grandeur of the American Republic, whose influence could not but increase, and Cyrus Harding, who had been much mixed up with the affairs of the Union, greatly interested his auditors by his recitals, his views, and his prognostics.

It chanced one day that Spilett was led to say,—

"But now, my dear Cyrus, all this industrial and commercial movement to which you predict a continual advance, does it not run the danger of being sooner or later completely stopped?"

"Stopped! And by what?"

"By the want of coal, which may justly be called the most precious of minerals."

"Yes, the most precious indeed," replied the engineer; "and it would seem that nature wished to prove that it was so by making the diamond, which is simply pure carbon crystallised."

"You don't mean to say, captain," interrupted Pencroft, "that we burn diamonds in our stoves in the shape of coal?"

"No, my friend," replied Harding.

"However," resumed Gideon Spilett, "you do not deny that some day the coal will be entirely consumed?"

"Oh! the veins of coal are still considerable, and the hundred thousand miners who annually extract from them a hundred millions of hundredweights have not nearly exhausted them."

"With the increasing consumption of coal," replied Gideon Spilett, "it can be foreseen that the hundred thousand workmen will soon become two hundred thousand, and that the rate of extraction will be doubled."

"Doubtless, but after the European mines, which will be soon worked more thoroughly with new machines, the American and

Australian mines will for a long time yet provide for the consumption in trade."

"For how long a time?" asked the reporter.

"For at least two hundred and fifty or three hundred years."

"That is reassuring for us, but a bad look-out for our great grandchildren!" observed Pencroft.

"They will discover something else," said Herbert.

"It is to be hoped so," answered Spilett, "for without coal there would be no machinery, and without machinery there would be no railways, no steamers, no manufactories, nothing of that which is indispensable to modern civilisation!"

"But what will they find?" asked Pencroft. "Can you guess, captain?"

"Nearly, my friend."

"And what will they burn instead of coal?"

"Water," replied Harding.

"Water!" cried Pencroft, "water as fuel for steamers and engines! water to heat water!"

"Yes, but water decomposed into its primitive elements," replied Cyrus Harding, "and decomposed, doubtless; by electricity, which will then have become a powerful and manageable force, for all great discoveries, by some inexplicable law, appear to agree and become complete at the same time. Yes, my friends, I believe that water will one day be employed as fuel, that hydrogen and oxygen which constitute it, used singly or together, will furnish an inexhaustible source of heat and light, of an intensity of which coal is not capable. Some day the coal-rooms of steamers and the tenders of locomotives will, instead of coal, be stored with these two condensed gases, which will burn in the furnaces with enormous calorific power. There is, therefore, nothing to fear. As long as the earth is inhabited it will supply the wants of its inhabitants, and there will be no want of either light or heat as long as the productions of the vegetable, mineral or animal kingdoms do not fail us. I believe, then, that when the deposits of coal are exhausted, we shall heat and warm ourselves with water. Water will be the coal of the future."

"I should like to see that," observed the sailor.

"You were born too soon, Pencroft," returned Neb, who only took part in the discussion by these words.

However, it was not Neb's speech which interrupted the conversation, but Top's barking, which broke out again with that strange intonation which had before perplexed the engineer. At the same time Top began to run round the mouth of the well, which opened at the extremity of the interior passage.

"What can Top be barking in that way for?" asked Pencroft.

"And Jup be growling like that?" added Herbert.

In fact the orang, joining the dog, gave unequivocal signs of agitation, and, singular to say, the two animals appeared more uneasy than angry.

"It is evident," said Gideon Spilett, "that this well is in direct communication with the sea, and that some marine animal comes from time to time to breathe at the bottom."

"That's evident," replied the sailor, "and there can be no other explanation to give. Quiet there, Top!" added Pencroft, turning to the dog, "and you, Jup, be off to your room!"

The ape and the dog were silent. Jup went off to bed, but Top remained in the room, and continued to utter low growls at intervals during the rest of the evening. There was no further talk on the subject, but the incident, however, clouded the brow of the engineer.

During the remainder of the month of July there was alternate rain and frost. The temperature was not so low as during the preceding winter, and its maximum did not exceed eight degrees Fahrenheit. But although this winter was less cold, it was more troubled by storms and squalls; the sea besides often endangered the safety of the Chimneys. At times it almost seemed as if an under-current raised these monstrous billows which thundered against the wall of Granite House.

When the settlers, leaning from their windows, gazed on the huge watery masses breaking beneath their eyes, they could not but admire the magnificent spectacle of the ocean in its impotent fury. The waves rebounded in dazzling foam, the beach entirely disappearing under the raging flood, and the cliff appearing to emerge from the sea itself, the spray rising to a height of more than a hundred feet.

During these storms it was difficult and even dangerous to venture out, owing to the frequently falling trees; however, the colonists never allowed a week to pass without having paid a visit to the corral. Happily this enclosure, sheltered by the south-eastern spur of Mount Franklin, did not greatly suffer from the violence of the hurricanes, which spared its trees, sheds, and palisades; but the poultry-yard on Prospect Heights, being directly exposed to the gusts of wind from the east, suffered considerable damage. The pigeon-house was twice unroofed and the paling blown down. All this required to be re-made more solidly than before, for, as may be clearly seen, Lincoln Island was situated in one of the most dangerous parts of the Pacific. It really appeared as if it formed the central point of vast cyclones, which beat it perpetually as the whip does the top, only here it was the top which was motionless and the whip which moved. During the first week of the month of August the weather became more moderate, and the atmosphere recovered the calm which it appeared to have lost for ever. With the calm the cold again became intense, and the thermometer fell to eight degrees Fahrenheit, below zero.

On the 3rd of August an excursion which had been talked of for several days was made into the south-eastern part of the island, towards Tadorn Marsh. The hunters were tempted by the aquatic game which took up their winter-quarters there. Wild duck, snipe, teal, and grebe, abounded there, and it was agreed that a day should be devoted to an expedition against these birds.

Not only Gideon Spilett and Herbert, but Pencroft and Neb also took part in this excursion. Cyrus Harding alone, alleging some work as an excuse, did not join them, but remained at Granite House.

The hunters proceeded in the direction of Port Balloon, in order to reach the marsh, after having promised to be back by the evening. Top and Jup accompanied them. As soon as they had passed over the Mercy Bridge, the engineer raised it and returned, intending to put into execution a project for the performance of which he wished to be alone.

Now this project was to minutely explore the interior well, the mouth of which was on a level with the passage of Granite House, and which communicated with the sea, since it formerly supplied a way to the waters of the lake.

Why did Top so often run round this opening? Why did he utter such strange barks when a sort of uneasiness seemed to draw him towards this well. Why did Jup join Top in a sort of common anxiety? Had this well branches besides the communication with the sea? Did it spread towards other parts of the island? This is what Cyrus Harding wished to know. He had resolved, therefore, to attempt the exploration of the well during the absence of his companions, and an opportunity for doing so had now presented itself.

It was easy to descend to the bottom of the well by employing the rope-ladder which had not been used since the establishment of the lift. The engineer drew the ladder to the hole, the diameter of which measured nearly six feet, and allowed it to unroll itself after having securely fastened its upper extremity. Then, having lighted a

86

lantern, taken a revolver, and placed a cutlass in his belt, he began the descent.

The sides were everywhere entire; but points of rock jutted out here and there, and by means of these points it would have been quite possible for an active creature to climb to the mouth of the well.

The engineer remarked this; but although he carefully examined these points by the light of his lantern, he could find no impression, no fracture which could give any reason to suppose that they had either recently or at any former time been used as a staircase. Cyrus Harding descended deeper, throwing the light of his lantern on all sides.

He saw nothing suspicious.

When the engineer had reached the last rounds he came upon the water, which was then perfectly calm. Neither at its level nor in any other part of the well, did any passage open which could lead to the interior of the cliff. The wall which Harding struck with the hilt of his cutlass sounded solid. It was compact granite, through which no living being could force a way. To arrive at the bottom of the well and then climb up to its mouth it was necessary to pass through the channel under the rocky sub-soil of the beach, which placed it in communication with the sea, and this was only possible for marine animals. As to the question of knowing where this channel ended, at what point of the shore, and at what depth beneath the water, it could not be answered.

Then Cyrus Harding, having ended his survey, re-ascended, drew up the ladder, covered the mouth of the well, and returned thoughtfully to the dining-room, saying to himself,—

"I have seen nothing, and yet there *is* something there!"

CHAPTER XII

**The Rigging of the Vessel—An Attack from Foxes—
Jup wounded—Jup cured—Completion of the Boat—
Pencroft's Triumph—The *Bonadventure's* trial Trip to the
South of the Island—An unexpected Document.**

In the evening the hunters returned, having enjoyed good
sport, and being literally loaded with game; indeed, they had as
much as four men could possibly carry. Top wore a necklace of teal
and Jup wreaths of snipe round his body.

"Here, master," cried Neb; "here's something to employ our
time! Preserved and made into pies we shall have a welcome store!
But I must have some one to help me. I count on you, Pencroft."

"No, Neb," replied the sailor; "I have the rigging of the vessel
to finish and to look after, and you will have to do without me."

"And you, Mr. Herbert?"

"I must go to the corral to-morrow, Neb," replied the lad.

"It will be you then, Mr. Spilett, who will help me?"

"To oblige you, Neb, I will," replied the reporter; "but I warn
you that if you disclose your receipts to me, I shall publish them."

"Whenever you like, Mr. Spilett," replied Neb; "whenever you
like."

And so the next day Gideon Spilett became Neb's assistant
and was installed in his culinary laboratory. The engineer had
previously made known to him the result of the exploration which
he had made the day before, and on this point the reporter shared
Harding's opinion, that although he had found nothing, a secret still
remained to be discovered!

The frost continued for another week, and the settlers did not
leave Granite House unless to look after the poultry-yard. The
dwelling was filled with appetising odours, which were emitted from
the learned manipulation of Neb and the reporter. But all the results
of the chase were not made into preserved provisions; and as the
game kept perfectly in the intense cold, wild duck and other fowl
were eaten fresh, and declared superior to all other aquatic birds in
the known world.

During this week Pencroft, aided by Herbert, who handled the
sail-maker's needle with much skill, worked with such energy that
the sails of that vessel were finished. There was no want of cordage.
Thanks to the rigging which had been recovered with the case of the
balloon, the ropes and cables from the net were all of good quality,

and the sailor turned them all to account. To the sails were attached strong bolt ropes, and there still remained enough from which to make the halliards, shrouds, and sheets, etc. The blocks were manufactured by Cyrus Harding under Pencroft's directions by means of the turning-lathe. It therefore happened that the rigging was entirely prepared before the vessel was finished. Pencroft also manufactured a flag, that flag so dear to every true American, containing the stars and stripes of their glorious Union. The colours for it were supplied from certain plants used in dyeing, and which were very abundant in the island; only to the thirty-seven stars, representing the thirty-seven States of the Union, which shine on the American flag, the sailor added a thirty-eighth, the star of "the State of Lincoln," for he considered his island as already united to the great republic. "And," said he, "it is so already in heart, if not in deed!"

In the meantime, the flag was hoisted at the central window of Granite House, and the settlers saluted it with three cheers.

The cold season was now almost at an end, and it appeared as if this second winter was to pass without any unusual occurrence, when, on the night of the 11th August, the plateau of Prospect Heights was menaced with complete destruction.

After a busy day the colonists were sleeping soundly, when towards four o'clock in the morning they were suddenly awakened by Top's barking.

The dog was not this time barking near the mouth of the well, but at the threshold of the door, at which he was scratching as if he wished to burst it open. Jup was also uttering piercing cries.

"Hallo, Top!" cried Neb, who was the first awake. But the dog continued to bark more furiously than ever.

"What's the matter now?" asked Harding.

And all dressing in haste rushed to the windows, which they opened.

Beneath their eyes was spread a sheet of snow which looked grey in the dim light. The settlers could see nothing, but they heard a singular yelping noise away in the darkness. It was evident that the beach had been invaded by a number of animals which could not be seen.

"What are they?" cried Pencroft.

"Wolves, jaguars, or apes?" replied Neb.

"They have nearly reached the plateau," said the reporter.

"And our poultry-yard," exclaimed Herbert, "and our garden!"

"Where can they have crossed?" asked Pencroft.

"They must have crossed the bridge on the shore," replied the engineer, "which one of us must have forgotten to close."

"True," said Spilett, "I remember to have left it open."

"A fine job you have made of it, Mr. Spilett," cried the sailor.

"What is done cannot be undone," replied Cyrus Harding. "We must consult what it will now be best to do."

Such were the questions and answers which were rapidly exchanged between Harding and his companions. It was certain that the bridge had been crossed, that the shore had been invaded by animals, and that whatever they might be they could by ascending the left bank of the Mercy reach Prospect Heights. They must therefore be advanced against quickly and fought with if necessary.

"But what are these beasts?" was asked a second time, as the yelpings were again heard more loudly than before. These yelps made Herbert start, and he remembered to have already heard them during his first visit to the sources of the Red Creek.

"They are culpeux foxes!" he exclaimed.

"Forward!" shouted the sailor.

And all arming themselves with hatchets, carbines, and revolvers, threw themselves into the lift and soon set foot on the shore.

Culpeux are dangerous animals when in great numbers and irritated by hunger, nevertheless the colonists did not hesitate to throw themselves into the midst of the troop, and their first shots vividly lighting up the darkness made their assailants draw back.

The chief thing was to hinder these plunderers from reaching the plateau, for the garden and the poultry-yard would then have been at their mercy, and immense, perhaps irreparable mischief, would inevitably be the result, especially with regard to the cornfield. But as the invasion of the plateau could only be made by the left bank of the Mercy, it was sufficient to oppose the culpeux on the narrow bank between the river and the cliff of granite.

This was plain to all, and, by Cyrus Harding's orders, they reached the spot indicated by him, while the culpeux rushed fiercely through the gloom. Harding, Gideon, Spilett, Herbert, Pencroft, and Neb posted themselves in impregnable line. Top, his formidable jaws open, preceded the colonists, and he was followed by Jup, armed with knotty cudgel, which he brandished like a club.

The night was extremely dark, it was only by the flashes from the revolvers as each person fired that they could see their assailants, who were at least a hundred in number, and whose eyes were glowing like hot coals.

"They must not pass!" shouted Pencroft.

"They shall not pass!" returned the engineer.

But if they did not pass it was not for want of having attempted it. Those in the rear pushed on the foremost assailants, and it was an incessant struggle with revolvers and hatchets. Several culpeux already lay dead on the ground, but their number did not appear to diminish, and it might have been supposed that reinforcements were continually arriving over the bridge.

The colonists were soon obliged to fight at close quarters, not without receiving some wounds, though happily very slight ones. Herbert had, with a shot from his revolver, rescued Neb, on whose back a culpeux had sprung like a tiger cat. Top fought with actual fury, flying at the throats of the foxes and strangling them instantaneously. Jup wielded his weapon valiantly, and it was in vain that they endeavoured to keep him in the rear. Endowed doubtless with sight which enabled him to pierce the obscurity, he was always in the thick of the fight, uttering from time to time a sharp hissing sound, which was with him the sign of great rejoicing.

At one moment he advanced so far, that by the light from a revolver he was seen surrounded by five or six large culpeux, with whom he was coping with great coolness.

However the struggle was ended at last, and victory was on the side of the settlers, but not until they had fought for two long hours! The first signs of the approach of day doubtless determined the retreat of their assailants, who scampered away towards the North, passing over the bridge, which Neb ran immediately to raise. When day had sufficiently lighted up the field of battle, the settlers counted as many as fifty dead bodies scattered about on the shore.

"And Jup!" cried Pencroft, "where is Jup?" Jup had disappeared. His friend Neb called him, and for the first time Jup did not reply to his friend's call.

Every one set out in search of Jup, trembling lest he should be found amongst the slain; they cleared the place of the bodies which stained the snow with their blood, Jup was found in the midst of a heap of culpeux, whose broken jaws and crushed bodies showed that they had to do with the terrible club of the intrepid animal.

Poor Jup still held in his hand the stump of his broken cudgel, but deprived of his weapon he had been overpowered by numbers, and his chest was covered with severe wounds.

"He is living," cried Neb, who was bending over him.

"And we will save him," replied the sailor. "We will nurse him as if he was one of ourselves."

It appeared as if Jup understood, for he leant his head on

Pencroft's shoulder as if to thank him. The sailor was wounded himself, but his wound was insignificant, as were those of his companions; for thanks to their firearms they had been almost always able to keep their assailants at a distance. It was therefore only the orang whose condition was serious.

Jup, carried by Neb and Pencroft, was placed in the lift, and only a slight moan now and then escaped his lips. He was gently drawn up to Granite House. There he was laid on a mattress taken from one of the beds, and his wounds were bathed with the greatest care. It did not appear that any vital part had been reached, but Jup was very weak from loss of blood, and a high fever soon set in after his wounds had been dressed. He was laid down, strict diet was imposed, "just like a real person," as Neb said, and they made him swallow several cups of a cooling drink, for which the ingredients were supplied from the vegetable medicine chest of Granite House. Jup was at first restless, but his breathing gradually became more regular, and he was left sleeping quietly. From time to time Top, walking on tip-toe, as one might say, came to visit his friend, and seemed to approve of all the care that had been taken of him. One of Jup's hands hung over the side of his bed, and Top licked it with a sympathising air.

They employed the day in interring the dead, who were dragged to the forest of the Far West, and there buried deep.

This attack, which might have had such serious consequences, was a lesson to the settlers, who from this time never went to bed until one of their number had made sure that all the bridges were raised, and that no invasion was possible.

However Jup, after having given them serious anxiety for several days, began to recover. His constitution brought him through, the fever gradually subsided, and Gideon Spilett, who was a bit of a doctor, pronounced him quite out of danger. On the 16th of August, Jup began to eat. Neb made him nice little sweet dishes, which the invalid discussed with great relish, for if he had a pet failing it was that of being somewhat of a gourmand, and Neb had never done anything to cure him of this fault.

"What would you have?" said he to Gideon Spilett, who sometimes expostulated with him for spoiling the ape. "Poor Jup has no other pleasure than that of the palate, and I am only too glad to be able to reward his services in this way!"

Ten days after having taken to his bed, on the 21st of August, Master Jup arose. His wounds were healed, and it was evident that he would not be long in regaining his usual strength and agility. Like all convalescents, he was tremendously hungry, and the reporter allowed him to eat as much as he liked, for he trusted to that instinct, which is too often wanting in reasoning beings, to keep the orang from any excess. Neb was delighted to see his pupil's appetite returning.

"Eat away, my Jup," said he, "and don't spare anything; you have shed your blood for us, and it is the least I can do to make you strong again!"

On the 25th of August Neb's voice was heard calling to his companions.

"Captain, Mr. Spilett, Mr. Herbert, Pencroft, come! come!"

The colonists, who were together in the dining-room, rose at Neb's call, who was then in Jup's room.

"What's the matter?" asked the reporter.

"Look," replied Neb, with a shout of laughter. And what did they see? Master Jup smoking calmly and seriously, sitting cross-legged like a Turk at the entrance to Granite House!

"My pipe," cried Pencroft. "He has taken my pipe! Hallo, my honest Jup, I make you a present of it! Smoke away, old boy, smoke away!"

And Jup gravely puffed out clouds of smoke which seemed to give him great satisfaction. Harding did not appear to be much astonished at this incident, and he cited several examples of tame apes, to whom the use of tobacco had become quite familiar.

But from this day Master Jup had a pipe of his own, the sailor's ex-pipe, which was hung in his room near his store of tobacco. He filled it himself, lighted it with a glowing coal, and appeared to be the happiest of quadrumana. It may readily be understood that this similarity of tastes of Jup and Pencroft served to tighten the bonds of friendship which already existed between the honest ape and the worthy sailor.

"Perhaps he is really a man," said Pencroft sometimes to Neb. "Should you be surprised to hear him beginning to speak to us some day?"

"My word, no," replied Neb. "What astonishes me is that he hasn't spoken to us before, for now he wants nothing but speech!"

"It would amuse me all the same," resumed the sailor, "if some fine day he said to me, 'Suppose we change pipes, Pencroft.'"

"Yes," replied Neb, "what a pity he was born dumb!"

With the month of September the winter ended, and the works were again eagerly commenced. The building of the vessel advanced rapidly, she was already completely decked over, and all the inside parts of the hull were firmly united with ribs bent by means of steam, which answered all the purposes of a mould.

As there was no want of wood, Pencroft proposed to the engineer to give a double lining to the hull, so as to completely insure the strength of the vessel.

Harding, not knowing what the future might have in store for them, approved the sailor's idea of making the craft as strong as possible. The interior and deck of the vessel was entirely finished towards the 15th of September. For calking the seams they made oakum of dry seaweed, which was hammered in between the planks; then these seams were covered with boiling tar, which was obtained in great abundance from the pines in the forest.

The management of the vessel was very simple. She had from the first been ballasted with heavy blocks of granite walled up, in a bed of lime, twelve thousand pounds of which they stowed away.

A deck was placed over this ballast, and the interior was divided into two cabins; two benches extended along them and served also as lockers. The foot of the mast supported the partition which separated the two cabins, which were reached by two hatchways let into the deck.

Pencroft had no trouble in finding a tree suitable for the mast. He chose a straight young fir, with no knots, and which he had only to square at the step, and round off at the top. The ironwork of the mast, the rudder and the hull, had been roughly but strongly forged at the Chimneys. Lastly, yards, masts, boom, spars, oars, etc., were all finished by the first week in October, and it was agreed that a trial trip should be taken round the island, so as to ascertain how the vessel would behave at sea, and how far they might depend upon her.

During all this time the necessary works had not been neglected. The corral was enlarged, for the flock of musmons and goats had been increased by a number of young ones, who had to be housed and fed. The colonists had paid visits also to the oyster bed, the warren, the coal and iron mines, and to the till then unexplored districts of the Far West forest, which abounded in game. Certain indigenous plants were discovered, and those fit for immediate use, contributed to vary the vegetable stores of Granite House.

They were a species of ficoide, some similar to those of the Cape, with eatable fleshy leaves, others bearing seeds containing a sort of flour.

On the 10th of October the vessel was launched. Pencroft was radiant with joy, the operation was perfectly successful; the boat completely rigged, having been pushed on rollers to the water's edge, was floated by the rising tide, amidst the cheers of the colonists, particularly of Pencroft, who showed no modesty on this occasion. Besides his importance was to last beyond the finishing of the vessel, since, after having built her, he was to command her. The grade of captain was bestowed upon him with the approbation of all. To satisfy Captain Pencroft, it was now necessary to give a name to the vessel, and, after many propositions had been discussed, the votes were all in favour of the *Bonadventure*. As soon as the *Bonadventure* had been lifted by the rising tide, it was seen that she lay evenly in the water, and would be easily navigated. However the trial trip was to be made that very day, by an excursion off the coast. The weather was fine, the breeze fresh, and the sea smooth, especially towards the south coast, for the wind was blowing from the north-west.

"All hands on board," shouted Pencroft, but breakfast was first necessary, and it was thought best to take provisions on board, in the event of their excursion being prolonged until the evening.

Cyrus Harding was equally anxious to try the vessel, the model of which had originated with him, although on the sailor's advice he had altered some parts of it, but he did not share Pencroft's confidence in her, and as the latter had not again spoken of the voyage to Tabor Island, Harding hoped he had given it up. He would have indeed great reluctance in letting two or three of his companions venture so far in so small a boat, which was not of more than fifteen tons' burden.

At half-past ten everybody was on board, even Top and Jup, and Herbert weighed the anchor, which was fast in the sand near the mouth of the Mercy. The sail was hoisted, the Lincolnian flag floated from the mast-head, and the *Bonadventure*, steered by Pencroft, stood out to sea.

The wind blowing out of Union Bay she ran before it, and thus showed her owners, much to their satisfaction, that she possessed a remarkably fast pair of heels, according to Pencroft's mode of speaking. After having doubled Flotsam Point and Claw Cape, the captain kept her close hauled, so as to sail along the southern coast of the island, when it was found she sailed admirably within five points of the wind. All hands were enchanted, they had a good vessel, which, in case of need, would be of great service to them, and with fine weather and a fresh breeze the voyage promised to be charming.

Pencroft now stood off the shore, three or four miles across from Port Balloon. The island then appeared in all its extent and under a new aspect, with the varied panorama of its shore from Claw Cape to Reptile End, the forests in which dark firs contrasted with the young foliage of other trees and overlooked the whole, and Mount Franklin whose lofty head was still whitened with snow.

"How beautiful it is!" cried Herbert.

"Yes, our island is beautiful and good," replied Pencroft. "I love it as I loved my poor mother. It received us poor and destitute, and now what is wanting to us five fellows who fell on it from the sky."

"Nothing," replied Neb; "nothing, captain."

And the two brave men gave three tremendous cheers in honour of their island!

During all this time Gideon Spilett, leaning against the mast, sketched the panorama which was developed before his eyes.

Cyrus Harding gazed on it in silence.

"Well, Captain Harding," asked Pencroft, "what do you think of our vessel?"

"She appears to behave well," replied the engineer.

"Good! And do you think now that she could undertake a voyage of some extent?"

"What voyage, Pencroft?"

"One to Tabor Island, for instance."

"My friend," replied Harding, "I think that in any pressing emergency we need not hesitate to trust ourselves to the *Bonadventure* even for a longer voyage; but you know I should see you set off to Tabor Island with great uneasiness, since nothing obliges you to go there."

"One likes to know one's neighbours," returned the sailor, who was obstinate in his idea. "Tabor Island is our neighbour, and the only one! Politeness requires us to go at least to pay a visit."

"By Jove," said Spilett; "our friend Pencroft has become very particular about the proprieties all at once!"

"I am not particular about anything at all," retorted the sailor; who was rather vexed by the engineer's opposition, but who did not wish to cause him anxiety.

"Consider, Pencroft," resumed Harding, "you cannot go alone to Tabor Island."

"One companion will be enough for me."

"Even so," replied the engineer, "you will risk depriving the colony of Lincoln Island of two settlers out of five."

"Out of six," answered Pencroft; "you forget Jup."

"Out of seven," added Neb; "Top is quite worth another."

"There is no risk at all in it, captain," replied Pencroft.

"That is possible, Pencroft; but I repeat it is to expose ourselves uselessly."

The obstinate sailor did not reply, and let the conversation drop, quite determined to resume it again. But he did not suspect that an incident would come to his aid and change into an act of humanity that which was at first only a doubtful whim.

After standing off the shore the *Bonadventure* again approached it in the direction of Port Balloon. It was important to ascertain the channels between the sandbanks and reefs, that buoys might be laid down, since this little creek was to be the harbour.

They were not more than half a mile from the coast, and it was necessary to tack to beat against the wind. The *Bonadventure* was then going at a very moderate rate, as the breeze, partly intercepted by the high land, scarcely swelled her sails, and the sea, smooth as glass, was only rippled now and then by passing gusts.

Herbert had stationed himself in the bows that he might indicate the course to be followed among the channels, when all at once he shouted,—

"Luff, Pencroft, luff!"

"What's the matter," replied the sailor, "a rock?"

"No—wait," said Herbert, "I don't quite see. Luff again—right—now."

So saying, Herbert leaning over the side, plunged his arm into the water and pulled it out, exclaiming,—

"A bottle!"

He held in his hand a corked bottle which he had just seized a few cables' length from the shore.

Cyrus Harding took the bottle Without uttering a single word he drew the cork, and took from it a damp paper, on which were written these words:—

"Castaway ... Tabor Island: 153° W long, 37° 11′ S lat.4"

CHAPTER XIII

Departure decided upon—Conjectures—Preparations—The three Passengers—First Night—Second Night—Tabor Island—Searching the Shore—Searching the Wood—No one—Animals—Plants—A Dwelling—Deserted.

"A castaway!" exclaimed Pencroft; "left on this Tabor Island not two hundred miles from us! Ah, Captain Harding, you won't now oppose my going."

"No, Pencroft," replied Cyrus Harding; "and you shall set out as soon as possible."

"To-morrow?"

"To-morrow!"

The engineer still held in his hand the paper which he had taken from the bottle. He contemplated it for some instants, then resumed,—

"From this document, my friends, from the way in which it is worded, we may conclude this: first, that the castaway on Tabor Island is a man possessing a considerable knowledge of navigation, since he gives the latitude and longitude of the island exactly as we ourselves found it, and to a second of approximation; secondly, that he is either English or American, as the document is written in the English language."

"That is perfectly logical," answered Spilett; "and the presence of this castaway explains the arrival of the case on the shores of our island. There must have been a wreck, since there is a castaway. As to the latter, whoever he may be, it is lucky for him that Pencroft thought of building this boat and of trying her this very day, for a day later and this bottle might have been broken on the rocks."

"Indeed," said Herbert, "it is a fortunate chance that the *Bonadventure* passed exactly where the bottle was still floating!"

"Does not this appear strange to you?" asked Harding of Pencroft.

"It appears fortunate, that's all," answered the sailor. "Do you see anything extraordinary in it, captain. The bottle must go somewhere, and why not here as well as anywhere else?"

"Perhaps you are right, Pencroft," replied the engineer; "and yet—"

"But," observed Herbert, "there's nothing to prove that this bottle has been floating long in the sea."

"Nothing," replied Gideon Spilett; "and the document appears even to have been recently written. What do you think about it, Cyrus?"

"It is difficult to say, and besides we shall soon know," replied Harding.

During this conversation Pencroft had not remained in-active. He had put the vessel about, and the *Bonadventure*, all sails set, was running rapidly towards Claw Cape.

Every one was thinking of the castaway on Tabor Island. Should they be in time to save him? This was a great event in the life of the colonists! They themselves were but castaways, but it was to be feared that another might not have been so fortunate, and their duty was to go to his succour.

Claw Cape was doubled, and about four o'clock the *Bonadventure* dropped her anchor at the mouth of the Mercy.

That same evening the arrangements for the new expedition were made. It appeared best that Pencroft and Herbert, who knew how to work the vessel, should undertake the voyage alone. By setting out the next day, the 10th of October, they would arrive on the 13th, for with the present wind it would not take more than forty-eight hours to make this passage of a hundred and fifty miles. One day in the island, three or four to return, they might hope therefore that on the 17th they would again reach Lincoln Island. The weather was fine, the barometer was rising, the wind appeared settled, everything then was in favour of these brave men whom an act of humanity was taking far from their island.

Thus it had been agreed that Cyrus Harding, Neb, and Gideon Spilett, should remain at Granite House, but an objection was raised, and Spilett, who had not forgotten his business as reporter to the *New York Herald*, having declared that he would go by swimming rather than lose such an opportunity, he was admitted to take a part in the voyage.

The evening was occupied in transporting on board the *Bonadventure* articles of bedding, utensils, arms, ammunition, a compass, provisions for a week, and this business being rapidly accomplished the colonists ascended to Granite House.

The next day, at five o'clock in the morning, the farewells were said, not without some emotion on both sides, and Pencroft setting sail made towards Claw Cape, which had to be doubled in order to proceed to the south-west.

The *Bonadventure* was already a quarter of a mile from the coast, when the passengers perceived on the heights of Granite

House two men waving their farewells; they were Cyrus Harding and Neb.

"Our friends," exclaimed Spilett, "this is our first separation for fifteen months."

Pencroft, the reporter, and Herbert waved in return, and Granite House soon disappeared behind the high rocks of the Cape.

During the first part of the day the *Bonadventure* was still in sight of the southern coast of Lincoln Island, which soon appeared just like a green basket, with Mount Franklin rising from the centre. The heights, diminished by distance, did not present an appearance likely to tempt vessels to touch there. Reptile End was passed in about an hour, though at a distance of about ten miles.

At this distance it was no longer possible to distinguish anything of the Western Coast, which stretched away to the ridges of Mount Franklin, and three hours after the last of Lincoln Island sank below the horizon.

The *Bonadventure* behaved capitally. Bounding over the waves she proceeded rapidly on her course. Pencroft had hoisted the foresail, and steering by the compass followed a rectilinear direction. From time to time Herbert relieved him at the helm, and the lad's hand was so firm that the sailor had not a point to find fault with.

Gideon Spilett chatted sometimes with one, sometimes with the other, if wanted he lent a hand with the ropes, and Captain Pencroft was perfectly satisfied with his crew.

In the evening the crescent moon, which would not be in its first quarter until the 16th, appeared in the twilight and soon set again. The night was dark but starry, and the next day again promised to be fine.

Pencroft prudently lowered the foresail, not wishing to be caught by a sudden gust while carrying too much canvas; it was perhaps an unnecessary precaution on such a calm night, but Pencroft was a prudent sailor and cannot be blamed for it.

The reporter slept part of the night. Pencroft and Herbert took turns for a spell of two hours each at the helm. The sailor trusted Herbert as he would himself, and his confidence was justified by the coolness and judgment of the lad. Pencroft gave him his directions as a commander to his steersman, and Herbert never allowed the *Bonadventure* to swerve even a point. The night passed quietly, as did the day of the 12th of October. A south-easterly direction was strictly maintained, unless the *Bonadventure* fell in with some unknown current she would come exactly within sight of Tabor Island.

As to the sea over which the vessel was then sailing, it was absolutely deserted. Now and then a great albatross or frigate bird passed within gun-shot, and Gideon Spilett wondered if it was to one of them that he had confided his last letter addressed to the *New York Herald*. These birds were the only beings that appeared to frequent this part of the ocean between Tabor and Lincoln Island.

"And yet," observed Herbert, "this is the time that whalers usually proceed towards the southern part of the Pacific. Indeed I do not think there could be a more deserted sea than this."

"It is not quite so deserted as all that," replied Pencroft.

"What do you mean," asked the reporter.

"We are on it. Do you take our vessel for a wreck and us for porpoises?"

And Pencroft laughed at his joke.

By the evening, according to calculation, it was thought that the *Bonadventure* had accomplished a distance of a hundred and twenty miles since her departure from Lincoln Island, that is to say in thirty-six hours, which would give her a speed of between three and four knots an hour. The breeze was very slight and might soon drop altogether. However it was hoped that the next morning by break of day, if the calculation had been correct and the course true, they would sight Tabor Island.

Neither Gideon Spilett, Herbert, nor Pencroft slept that night. In the expectation of the next day they could not but feel some emotion. There was so much uncertainty in their enterprise! Were they near Tabor Island? Was the island still inhabited by the castaway to whose succour they had come. Who was this man? Would not his presence disturb the little colony till then so united? Besides, would he be content to exchange his prison for another? All these questions, which would no doubt be answered the next day, kept them in suspense, and at the dawn of day they all fixed their gaze on the western horizon.

"Land!" shouted Pencroft at about six o'clock in the morning.

And it was impossible that Pencroft should be mistaken, it was evident that land was there. Imagine the joy of the little crew of the *Bonadventure*. In a few hours they would land on the beach of the island!

The low coast of Tabor Island, scarcely emerging from the sea, was not more than fifteen miles distant.

The head of the *Bonadventure*, which was a little to the south of the island, was set directly towards it, and as the sun mounted in the east, his rays fell upon one or two headlands.

"This is a much less important isle than Lincoln Island," observed Herbert, "and is probably due like ours to some submarine convulsion."

At eleven o'clock the *Bonadventure* was not more than two miles off, and Pencroft, whilst looking for a suitable place at which to land, proceeded very cautiously through the unknown waters. The whole of the island could now be surveyed, and on it could be seen groups of gum and other large trees, of the same species as those growing on Lincoln Island. But the astonishing thing was that no smoke arose to show that the island was inhabited, not a signal appeared on any point of the shore whatever!

And yet the document was clear enough; there was a castaway, and this castaway should have been on the watch.

In the meanwhile the *Bonadventure* entered the winding channels among the reefs, and Pencroft observed every turn with extreme care. He had put Herbert at the helm, posting himself in the bows, inspecting the water, whilst he held the halliard in his hand, ready to lower the sail at a moment's notice. Gideon Spilett with his glass eagerly scanned the shore, though without perceiving anything.

However at about twelve o'clock the keel of the *Bonadventure* grated on the bottom. The anchor was let go, the sails furled, and the crew of the little vessel landed.

And there was no reason to doubt that this was Tabor Island, since according to the most recent charts there was no island in this part of the Pacific between New Zealand and the American coast.

The vessel was securely moored, so that there should be no danger of her being carried away by the receding tide; then Pencroft and his companions, well armed, ascended the shore, so as to gain an elevation of about two hundred and fifty or three hundred feet which rose at a distance of half a mile.

"From the summit of that hill," said Spilett, "we can no doubt obtain a complete view of the island, which will greatly facilitate our search."

"So as to do here," replied Herbert, "that which Captain Harding did the very first thing on Lincoln Island, by climbing Mount Franklin."

"Exactly so," answered the reporter; "and it is the best plan of proceeding."

Whilst thus talking the explorers had advanced along a clearing which terminated at the foot of the hill. Flocks of rock-pigeons and sea-swallows, similar to those of Lincoln Island, fluttered around them. Under the woods which skirted the glade on the left they could hear the bushes rustling and see the grass waving, which indicated the presence of timid animals, but still nothing to show that the island was inhabited.

Arrived at the foot of the hill, Pencroft, Spilett, and Herbert climbed it in a few minutes, and gazed anxiously round the horizon.

They were on an islet which did not measure more than six miles in circumference, its shape not much bordered by capes or promontories, bays or creeks, being a lengthened oval. All around, the lonely sea extended to the limits of the horizon. No land nor even a sail was in sight.

This woody islet did not offer the varied aspects of Lincoln Island, arid and wild in one part, but fertile and rich in the other. On the contrary this was a uniform mass of verdure, out of which rose two or three hills of no great height. Obliquely to the oval of the island ran a stream through a wide meadow falling into the sea on the west by a narrow mouth.

"The domain is limited," said Herbert.

"Yes," rejoined Pencroft. "It would have been too small for us."

"And moreover," said the reporter, "it appears to be uninhabited."

"Indeed," answered Herbert, "nothing here betrays the presence of man."

"Let us go down," said Pencroft, "and search."

The sailor and his two companions returned to the shore, to the place where they had left the *Bonadventure*.

They had decided to make the tour of the island on foot, before exploring the interior, so that not a spot should escape their investigations. The beach was easy to follow, and only in some places was their way barred by large rocks, which, however, they easily passed round. The explorers proceeded towards the south, disturbing numerous flocks of sea-birds and herds of seals, which threw themselves into the sea as soon as they saw the strangers at a distance.

"Those beasts yonder," observed the reporter, "do not see men for the first time. They fear them, therefore they must know them."

An hour after their departure they arrived on the southern point of the islet, terminated by a sharp cape, and proceeded towards the north along the western coast, equally formed by sand and rocks, the background bordered with thick woods.

There was not a trace of a habitation in any part, not the print of a human foot on the shore of the island, which after four hours' walking had been gone completely round.

103

It was to say the least very extraordinary, and they were compelled to believe that Tabor Island was not or was no longer inhabited. Perhaps, after all, the document was already several months or several years old, and it was possible in this case, either that the castaway had been enabled to return to his country, or that he had died of misery.

Pencroft, Spilett, and Herbert, forming more or less probable conjectures, dined rapidly on board the *Bonadventure*, so as to be able to continue their excursion until nightfall. This was done at five o'clock in the evening, at which hour they entered the wood.

Numerous animals fled at their approach, being principally, one might say, only goats and pigs, which it was easy to see belonged to European species.

Doubtless some whaler had landed them on the island, where they had rapidly increased. Herbert resolved to catch one or two living, and take them back to Lincoln Island.

It was no longer doubtful that men at some period or other had visited this islet, and this became still more evident when paths appeared trodden through the forest, felled trees, and everywhere traces of the hand of man; but the trees were becoming rotten, and had been felled many years ago; the marks of the axe were velveted with moss, and the grass grew long and thick on the paths, so that it was difficult to find them.

"But," observed Gideon Spilett, "this not only proves that men have landed on the island, but also that they lived on it for some time. Now, who were these men? How many of them remain?"

"The document," said Herbert, "only spoke of one castaway."

"Well, if he is still on the island," replied Pencroft, "it is impossible but that we shall find him."

The exploration was continued. The sailor and his companions naturally followed the route which cut diagonally across the island, and they were thus obliged to follow the stream which flowed towards the sea.

If the animals of European origin, if works due to a human hand, showed incontestably that men had already visited the island, several specimens of the vegetable kingdom did not prove it less. In some places, in the midst of clearings, it was evident that the soil had been planted with culinary plants, at probably the same distant period.

What, then, was Herbert's joy, when he recognised potatoes, chicory, sorrel, carrots, cabbages, and turnips, of which it was sufficient to collect the seed to enrich the soil of Lincoln Island.

"Capital, jolly!" exclaimed Pencroft. "That will suit Neb as well

104

as us. Even if we do not find the castaway, at least our voyage will not have been useless, and God will have rewarded us."

"Doubtless," replied Gideon Spilett; "but to see the state in which we find these plantations, it is to be feared that the island has not been inhabited for some time."

"Indeed," answered Herbert, "an inhabitant, whoever he was, could not have neglected such an important culture!"

"Yes," said Pencroft, "the castaway has gone."

"We must suppose so."

"It must then be admitted that the document has already a distant date?"

"Evidently."

"And that the bottle only arrived at Lincoln Island after having floated in the sea a long time."

"Why not," returned Pencroft. "But night is coming on," added he, "and I think that it will be best to give up the search for the present."

"Let us go on board, and to-morrow we will begin again," said the reporter.

This was the wisest course, and it was about to be followed when Herbert, pointing to a confused mass among the trees, exclaimed,—

"A hut!"

All three immediately ran towards the dwelling. In the twilight it was just possible to see that it was built of planks and covered with a thick tarpaulin.

The half-closed door was pushed open by Pencroft, who entered with a rapid step.

The hut was empty!

CHAPTER XIV

The Inventory—Night—A few Letters—Continuation of the Search—Plants and Animals—Herbert in great Danger—On Board—The Departure—Bad Weather—A Gleam of Reason—Lost on the Sea—A timely Light.

Pencroft, Herbert, and Gideon Spilett remained silent in the midst of the darkness.

Pencroft shouted loudly.

No reply was made.

The sailor then struck a light and set fire to a twig. This lighted for a minute a small room, which appeared perfectly empty. At the back was a rude fireplace, with a few cold cinders, supporting an armful of dry wood. Pencroft threw the blazing twig on it, the wood cracked and gave forth a bright light.

The sailor and his two companions then perceived a disordered bed, of which the damp and yellow coverlets proved that it had not been used for a long time. In the corner of the fireplace were two kettles, covered with rust, and an overthrown pot. A cupboard, with a few mouldy sailor's clothes; on the table a tin plate and a Bible, eaten away by damp; in a corner a few tools, a spade, pickaxe, two fowling-pieces, one of which was broken; on a plank, forming a shelf, stood a barrel of powder, still untouched, a barrel of shot, and several boxes of caps, all thickly covered with dust, accumulated, perhaps, by many long years.

"There is no one here," said the reporter.

"No one," replied Pencroft.

"It is a long time since this room has been inhabited," observed Herbert.

"Yes, a very long time!" answered the reporter.

"Mr. Spilett," then said Pencroft, "instead of returning on board, I think that it would be well to pass the night in this hut."

"You are right, Pencroft," answered Gideon Spilett, "and if its owner returns, well! perhaps he will not be sorry to find the place taken possession of."

"He will not return," said the sailor, shaking his head.

"You think that he has quitted the island?" asked the reporter.

"If he had quitted the island he would have taken away his weapons and his tools," replied Pencroft. "You know the value which castaways set on such articles as these, the last remains of a wreck? No! no!" repeated the sailor, in a tone of conviction, "no, he

106

has not left the island! If he had escaped in a boat made by himself, he would still less have left these indispensable and necessary articles. No! he is on the island!"

"Living?" asked Herbert.

"Living or dead. But if he is dead, I suppose he has not buried himself, and so we shall at least find his remains!"

It was then agreed that the night should be passed in the deserted dwelling, and a store of wood found in a corner was sufficient to warm it. The door closed, Pencroft, Herbert, and Spilett remained there, seated on a bench, talking little but wondering much. They were in a frame of mind to imagine anything or expect anything. They listened eagerly for sounds outside. The door might have opened suddenly, and a man presented himself to them without their being in the least surprised, notwithstanding all that the hut revealed of abandonment, and they had their hands ready to press the hands of this man, this castaway, this unknown friend, for whom friends were waiting.

But no voice was heard, the door did not open. The hours thus passed away.

How long the night appeared to the sailor and his companions! Herbert alone slept for two hours, for at his age sleep is a necessity. They were all three anxious to continue their exploration of the day before, and to search the most secret recesses of the islet! The inferences deduced by Pencroft were perfectly reasonable, and it was nearly certain that, as the hut was deserted, and the tools, utensils, and weapons were still there, the owner had succumbed. It was agreed, therefore, that they should search for his remains, and give them at least Christian burial.

Day dawned; Pencroft and his companions immediately proceeded to survey the dwelling. It had certainly been built in a favourable situation, at the back of a little hill, sheltered by five or six magnificent gum trees. Before its front and through the trees the axe had prepared a wide clearing, which allowed the view to extend to the sea. Beyond a lawn, surrounded by a wooden fence falling to pieces, was the shore, on the left of which was the mouth of the stream.

The hut had been built of planks, and it was easy to see that these planks had been obtained from the hull or deck of a ship. It was probable that a disabled vessel had been cast on the coast of the island, that one at least of the crew had been saved, and that by means of the wreck this man, having tools at his disposal, had built the dwelling.

And this became still more evident when Gideon Spilett, after

107

having walked round the hut, saw on a plank, probably one of those which had formed the armour of the wrecked vessel, these letters already half effaced:—

"Br—tan—a."

"Britannia," exclaimed Pencroft, whom the reporter had called; "it is a common name for ships, and I could not say if she was English or American!"

"It matters very little, Pencroft!"

"Very little indeed," answered the sailor; "and we will save the survivor of her crew if he is still living, to whatever country he may belong. But before beginning our search again let us go on board the *Bonadventure*."

A sort of uneasiness had seized Pencroft upon the subject of his vessel. Should the island be inhabited after all, and should some one have taken possession of her? But he shrugged his shoulders at such an unreasonable supposition. At any rate the sailor was not sorry to go to breakfast on board. The road already trodden was not long, scarcely a mile. They set out on their walk, gazing into the wood and thickets through which goats and pigs fled in hundreds.

Twenty minutes after leaving the hut Pencroft and his companions reached the western coast of the island, and saw the *Bonadventure* held fast by her anchor, which was buried deep in the sand.

Pencroft could not restrain a sigh of satisfaction. After all this vessel was his child, and it is the right of fathers to be often uneasy when there is no occasion for it.

They returned on board, breakfasted, so that it should not be necessary to dine until very late; then the repast being ended, the exploration was continued and conducted with the most minute care. Indeed, it was very probable that the only inhabitant of the island had perished. It was therefore more for the traces of a dead than of a living man that Pencroft and his companions searched. But their searches were vain, and during the half of that day they sought to no purpose among the thickets of trees which covered the islet. There was then scarcely any doubt that, if the castaway was dead, no trace of his body now remained, but that some wild beast had probably devoured it to the last bone.

"We will set off to-morrow at daybreak," said Pencroft to his two companions, as about two o'clock they were resting for a few minutes under the shade of a clump of firs.

"I should think that we might without scruple take the utensils which belonged to the castaway," added Herbert.

"I think so too," returned Gideon Spilett; "and these arms and tools will make up the stores of Granite House. The supply of powder and shot is also most important."

"Yes," replied Pencroft; "but we must not forget to capture a couple or two of those pigs, of which Lincoln Island is destitute—"

"Nor to gather those seeds," added Herbert, "which will give us all the vegetables of the Old and the New Worlds."

"Then perhaps it would be best," said the reporter, "to remain a day longer on Tabor Island, so as to collect all that may be useful to us."

"No, Mr. Spilett," answered Pencroft, "I will ask you to set off to-morrow at daybreak. The wind seems to me to be likely to shift to the west, and after having had a fair wind for coming we shall have a fair wind for going back."

"Then do not let us lose time," said Herbert, rising.

"We won't waste time," returned Pencroft. "You, Herbert, go and gather the seeds, which you know better than we do. Whilst you do that, Mr. Spilett and I will go and have a pig hunt, and even without Top I hope we shall manage to catch a few!"

Herbert accordingly took the path which led towards the cultivated part of the islet, whilst the sailor and the reporter entered the forest.

Many specimens of the porcine race fled before them, and these animals, which were singularly active, did not appear to be in a humour to allow themselves to be approached.

However, after an hour's chase, the hunters had just managed to get hold of a couple lying in a thicket, when cries were heard resounding from the north part of the island. With the cries were mingled terrible yells, in which there was nothing human.

Pencroft and Gideon Spilett were at once on their feet, and the pigs by this movement began to run away, at the moment when the sailor was getting ready the rope to bind them.

"That's Herbert's voice," said the reporter.

"Run!" exclaimed Pencroft.

And the sailor and Spilett immediately ran at full speed towards the spot from whence the cries proceeded.

They did well to hasten, for at a turn of the path near a clearing they saw the lad thrown on the ground and in the grasp of a savage being, apparently a gigantic ape, who was about to do him some great harm.

To rush on this monster, throw him on the ground in his turn, snatch Herbert from him, then bind him securely, was the work of a minute for Pencroft and Gideon Spilett. The sailor was of Herculean strength, the reporter also very powerful, and in spite of the monster's resistance he was firmly tied so that he could not even move.

"You are not hurt, Herbert," asked Spilett.

"No, no!"

"Oh, if this ape had wounded him!" exclaimed Pencroft.

"But he is not an ape," answered Herbert.

At these words Pencroft and Gideon Spilett looked at the singular being who lay on the ground. Indeed it was not an ape, it was a human being, a man. But what a man! A savage in all the horrible acceptation of the word, and so much the more frightful that he seemed fallen to the lowest degree of brutishness!

Shaggy hair, untrimmed beard descending to the chest, the body almost naked except a rag round the waist, wild eyes, enormous hands with immensely long nails, skin the colour of mahogany, feet as hard as if made of horn,—such was the miserable creature who yet had a claim to be called a man. But it might justly be asked if there were yet a soul in this body, or if the brute instinct alone survived in it!

"Are you quite sure that this is a man, or that he has ever been one?" said Pencroft to the reporter.

"Alas! there is no doubt about it," replied Spilett.

"Then this must be the castaway?" asked Herbert.

"Yes," replied Gideon Spilett, "but the unfortunate man has no longer anything human about him!"

The reporter spoke the truth. It was evident that if the castaway had ever been a civilised being, solitude had made him a savage, or worse, perhaps a regular man of the woods. Hoarse sounds issued from his throat between his teeth, which were sharp as the teeth of a wild beast made to tear raw flesh.

Memory must have deserted him long before, and for a long time also he had forgotten how to use his gun and tools, and he no longer knew how to make a fire! It could be seen that he was active and powerful, but the physical qualities had been developed in him to the injury of the moral qualities. Gideon Spilett spoke to him. He did not appear to understand or even to hear. And yet on looking into his eyes, the reporter thought he could see that all reason was not extinguished in him. However, the prisoner did not struggle, nor even attempt to break his bonds. Was he overwhelmed by the presence of men whose fellow he had once been? Had he found in some corner of his brain a fleeting remembrance which recalled him to humanity? If free, would he attempt to fly, or would he remain? They could not tell, but they did not make the experiment; and after gazing attentively at the miserable creature,—

"Whoever he may be," remarked Gideon Spilett; "whoever he may have been, and whatever he may become, it is our duty to take him with us to Lincoln Island."

"Yes, yes!" replied Herbert; "and perhaps with care we may arouse in him some gleam of intelligence."

"The soul does not die," said the reporter; "and it would be a great satisfaction to rescue one of God's creatures from brutishness."

Pencroft shook his head doubtfully.

"We must try at any rate," returned the reporter; "humanity commands us."

It was indeed their duty as Christians and civilised beings. All three felt this, and they well knew that Cyrus Harding would approve of their acting thus.

"Shall we leave him bound?" asked the sailor.

"Perhaps he would walk if his feet were unfastened," said Herbert.

"Let us try," replied Pencroft.

The cords which shackled the prisoner's feet were cut off, but his arms remained securely fastened. He got up by himself and did not manifest any desire to run away. His hard eyes darted a piercing glance at the three men, who walked near him, but nothing denoted that he recollected being their fellow, or at least having been so. A continual hissing sound issued from his lips, his aspect was wild, but he did not attempt to resist.

By the reporter's advice the unfortunate man was taken to the hut. Perhaps the sight of the things that belonged to him would make some impression on him! Perhaps a spark would be sufficient to revive his obscured intellect, to rekindle his dulled soul. The dwelling was not far off. In a few minutes they arrived there, but the prisoner remembered nothing, and it appeared that he had lost consciousness of everything.

What could they think of the degree of brutishness into which this miserable being had fallen, unless that his imprisonment on the islet dated from a very distant period, and after having arrived there a rational being solitude had reduced him to this condition.

The reporter then thought that perhaps the sight of fire would have some effect on him, and in a moment one of those beautiful flames, that attract even animals, blazed up on the hearth. The sight of the flame seemed at first to fix the attention of the unhappy object, but soon he turned away and the look of intelligence faded. Evidently there was nothing to be done, for the time at least, but to

111

take him on board the *Bonadventure*. This was done, and he remained there in Pencroft's charge.

Herbert and Spilett returned to finish their work; and some hours after they came back to the shore, carrying the utensils and guns, a store of vegetables, of seeds, some game, and two couple of pigs.

All was embarked, and the *Bonadventure* was ready to weigh anchor and sail with the morning tide.

The prisoner had been placed in the fore cabin, where he remained quiet, silent, apparently deaf and dumb.

Pencroft offered him something to eat, but he pushed away the cooked meat that was presented to him and which doubtless did not suit him. But on the sailor showing him one of the ducks which Herbert had killed, he pounced on it like a wild beast, and devoured it greedily.

"You think that he will recover his senses?" asked Pencroft. "It is not impossible that our care will have an effect upon him, for it is solitude that has made him what he is, and from this time forward he will be no longer alone."

"The poor man must no doubt have been in this state for a long time," said Herbert.

"Perhaps," answered Gideon Spilett.

"About what age is he?" asked the lad.

"It is difficult to say," replied the reporter; "for it is impossible to see his features under the thick beard which covers his face; but he is no longer young, and I suppose he might be about fifty."

"Have you noticed, Mr. Spilett, how deeply sunk his eyes are?" asked Herbert.

"Yes, Herbert; but I must add that they are more human than one could expect from his appearance."

"However, we shall see," replied Pencroft; "and I am anxious to know what opinion Captain Harding will have of our savage. We went to look for a human creature, and we are bringing back a monster! After all we did what we could."

The night passed, and whether the prisoner slept or not could not be known; but at any rate, although he had been unbound, he did not move. He was like a wild animal, which appears stunned at first by its capture, and becomes wild again afterwards.

At daybreak the next morning, the 15th of October, the change of weather predicted by Pencroft occurred. The wind having shifted to the north-west favoured the return of the *Bonadventure*, but at the same time it freshened, which would render navigation more difficult.

At five o'clock in the morning the anchor was weighed. Pencroft took a reef in the mainsail, and steered towards the north-east, so as to sail straight for Lincoln Island.

The first day of the voyage was not marked by any incident. The prisoner remained quiet in the fore-cabin, and as he had been a sailor it appeared that the motion of the vessel might produce on him a salutary reaction. Did some recollection of his former calling return to him? However that might be he remained tranquil, astonished rather than depressed.

The next day the wind increased, blowing more from the north, consequently in a less favourable direction for the *Bonadventure*. Pencroft was soon obliged to sail close-hauled, and without saying anything about it he began to be uneasy at the state of the sea, which frequently broke over the bows. Certainly, if the wind did not moderate, it would take a longer time to reach Lincoln Island than it had taken to make Tabor Island.

Indeed, on the morning of the 17th, the *Bonadventure* had been forty-eight hours at sea, and nothing showed that she was near the island. It was impossible, besides, to estimate the distance traversed, or to trust to the reckoning for the direction, as the speed had been very irregular.

Twenty-four hours after there was yet no land in sight. The wind was right ahead and the sea very heavy. The sails were close-reefed, and they tacked frequently. On the 18th, a wave swept completely over the *Bonadventure;* and if the crew had not taken the precaution of lashing themselves to the deck, they would have been carried away.

On this occasion Pencroft and his companions, who were occupied with loosing themselves, received unexpected aid from the prisoner, who emerged from the hatchway as if his sailor's instinct had suddenly returned, broke a piece out of the bulwarks with a spar so as to let the water which filled the deck escape. Then the vessel being clear, he descended to his cabin without having uttered a word. Pencroft, Gideon Spilett, and Herbert, greatly astonished, let him proceed.

Their situation was truly serious, and the sailor had reason to fear that he was lost on the wide sea without any possibility of recovering his course.

The night was dark and cold. However, about eleven o'clock, the wind fell, the sea went down, and the speed of the vessel, as she laboured less, greatly increased.

Neither Pencroft, Spilett, nor Herbert thought of taking an hour's sleep. They kept a sharp look-out, for either Lincoln Island could not be far distant and would be sighted at daybreak, or the *Bonadventure*, carried away by currents, had drifted so much that it would be impossible to rectify her course. Pencroft, uneasy to the last degree, yet did not despair, for he had a gallant heart, and grasping the tiller he anxiously endeavoured to pierce the darkness which surrounded them.

About two o'clock in the morning he started forward,—

"A light! a light!" he shouted.

Indeed, a bright light appeared twenty miles to the north-east. Lincoln Island was there, and this fire, evidently lighted by Cyrus Harding, showed them the course to be followed. Pencroft, who was bearing too much to the north, altered his course and steered towards the fire, which burned brightly above the horizon like a star of the first magnitude.

CHAPTER XV

The Return—Discussion—Cyrus Harding and the Stranger—Port Balloon—The Engineer's Devotion—A touching Incident—Tears flow.

The next day, the 20th of October, at seven o'clock in the morning, after a voyage of four days, the *Bonadventure* gently glided up to the beach at the mouth of the Mercy.

Cyrus Harding and Neb, who had become very uneasy at the bad weather and the prolonged absence of their companions, had climbed at daybreak to the plateau of Prospect Heights, and they had at last caught sight of the vessel which had been so long in returning.

"God be praised! there they are!" exclaimed Cyrus Harding.

As to Neb in his joy, he began to dance, to twirl round, clapping his hands and shouting, "Oh! my master!" A more touching pantomime than the finest discourse.

The engineer's first idea, on counting the people on the deck of the *Bonadventure*, was that Pencroft had not found the castaway of Tabor Island, or at any rate that the unfortunate man had refused to leave his island and change one prison for another.

Indeed Pencroft, Gideon Spilett, and Herbert were alone on the deck of the *Bonadventure*.

The moment the vessel touched, the engineer and Neb were waiting on the beach, and before the passengers had time to leap on to the sand, Harding said: "We have been very uneasy at your delay, my friends! Did you meet with any accident?"

"No," replied Gideon Spilett; "on the contrary, everything went wonderfully well. We will tell you all about it."

"However," returned the engineer, "your search has been unsuccessful, since you are only three just as you went!"

"Excuse me, captain," replied the sailor, "we are four."

"You have found the castaway?"

"Yes."

"And you have brought him?"

"Yes."

"Living?"

"Yes."

"Where is he? Who is he?"

"He is," replied the reporter, "or rather he was, a man! There, Cyrus, that is all we can tell you!"

115

The engineer was then informed of all that had passed during the voyage, and under what conditions the search had been conducted; how the only dwelling in the island had long been abandoned; how at last a castaway had been captured, who appeared no longer to belong to the human species.

"And that's just the point," added Pencroft, "I don't know if we have done right to bring him here."

"Certainly you have, Pencroft," replied the engineer quickly.

"But the wretched creature has no sense!"

"That is possible at present," replied Cyrus Harding; "but only a few months ago the wretched creature was a man like you and me. And who knows what will become of the survivor of us after a long solitude on this island? It is a great misfortune to be alone, my friends; and it must be believed that solitude can quickly destroy reason, since you have found this poor creature in such a state!"

"But, captain," asked Herbert, "what leads you to think that the brutishness of the unfortunate man began only a few months back?"

"Because the document we found had been recently written," answered the engineer, "and the castaway alone can have written it."

"Always supposing," observed Gideon Spilett, "that it had not been written by a companion of this man, since dead."

"That is impossible, my dear Spilett."

"Why so?" asked the reporter.

"Because the document would then have spoken of two castaways," replied Harding, "and it mentioned only one."

Herbert then in a few words related the incidents of the voyage, and dwelt on the curious fact of the sort of passing gleam in the prisoner's mind, when for an instant in the height of the storm he had become a sailor.

"Well, Herbert," replied the engineer, "you are right to attach great importance to this fact. The unfortunate man cannot be incurable, and despair has made him what he is; but here he will find his fellow-men, and since there is still a soul in him, this soul we shall save!"

The castaway of Tabor Island, to the great pity of the engineer and the great astonishment of Neb, was then brought from the cabin which he occupied in the fore part of the *Bonadventure*; when once on land he manifested a wish to run away.

But Cyrus Harding approaching, placed his hand on his shoulder with a gesture full of authority, and looked at him with infinite tenderness. Immediately the unhappy man, submitting to a superior will, gradually became calm, his eyes fell, his head bent, and he made no more resistance.

"Poor fellow!" murmured the engineer.

Cyrus Harding had attentively observed him. To judge by his appearance this miserable being had no longer anything human about him, and yet Harding, as had the reporter already, observed in his look an indefinable trace of intelligence.

It was decided that the castaway, or rather the stranger, as he was thenceforth termed by his companions, should live in one of the rooms of Granite House, from which, however, he could not escape. He was led there without difficulty; and with careful attention, it might, perhaps, be hoped that some day he would be a companion to the settlers in Lincoln Island.

Cyrus Harding, during breakfast, which Neb had hastened to prepare, as the reporter, Herbert, and Pencroft were dying of hunger, heard in detail all the incidents which had marked the voyage of exploration to the islet. He agreed with his friends on this point, that the stranger must be either English or American, the name Britannia leading them to suppose this, and, besides, through the bushy beard, and under the shaggy, matted hair, the engineer thought he could recognise the characteristic features of the Anglo-Saxon.

"But, by the bye," said Gideon Spilett, addressing Herbert, "you never told us how you met this savage, and we know nothing, except that you would have been strangled, if we had not happened to come up in time to help you!"

"Upon my word," answered Herbert, "it is rather difficult to say how it happened. I was, I think, occupied in collecting my plants, when I heard a noise like an avalanche falling from a very tall tree. I scarcely had time to look round. This unfortunate man, who was without doubt concealed in a tree, rushed upon me in less time than I take to tell you about it, and unless Mr. Spilett and Pencroft—"

"My boy!" said Cyrus Harding, "you ran a great danger, but, perhaps, without that, the poor creature would have still hidden himself from your search, and we should not have had a new companion."

"You hope, then, Cyrus, to succeed in reforming the man?" asked the reporter.

"Yes," replied the engineer.

Breakfast over, Harding and his companions left Granite House and returned to the beach. They there occupied themselves in unloading the *Bonadventure*, and the engineer, having examined the arms and tools, saw nothing which could help them to establish the identity of the stranger.

The capture of pigs, made on the islet, was looked upon as being very profitable to Lincoln Island, and the animals were led to the sty, where they soon became at home.

The two barrels, containing the powder and shot, as well as the box of caps, were very welcome. It was agreed to establish a small powder-magazine, either outside Granite House or in the Upper Cavern, where there would be no fear of explosion. However, the use of pyroxyle was to be continued, for this substance giving excellent results, there was no reason for substituting ordinary powder.

When the unloading of the vessel was finished,—

"Captain," said Pencroft, "I think it would be prudent to put our *Bonadventure* in a safe place."

"Is she not safe at the mouth of the Mercy?" asked Cyrus Harding.

"No, captain," replied the sailor. "Half of the time she is stranded on the sand, and that works her. She is a famous craft, you see, and she behaved admirably during the squall which struck us on our return."

"Could she not float in the river?"

"No doubt, captain, she could; but there is no shelter there, and in the east winds, I think that the *Bonadventure* would suffer much from the surf."

"Well, where would you put her, Pencroft?"

"In Port Balloon," replied the sailor. "That little creek, shut in by rocks, seems to me to be just the harbour we want."

"Is it not rather far?"

"Pooh! it is not more than three miles from Granite House, and we have a fine straight road to take us there!"

"Do it then, Pencroft, and take your *Bonadventure* there," replied the engineer, "and yet I would rather have her under our more immediate protection. When we have time, we must make a little harbour for her."

"Famous!" exclaimed Pencroft. "A harbour with a lighthouse, a pier, and a dock! Ah! really with you, captain, everything becomes easy."

"Yes, my brave Pencroft," answered the engineer, "but on condition, however, that you help me, for you do as much as three men in all our work."

Herbert and the sailor then re-embarked on board the *Bonadventure*, the anchor was weighed, the sail hoisted, and the wind drove her rapidly towards Claw Cape. Two hours after, she was reposing on the tranquil waters of Port Balloon.

During the first days passed by the stranger in Granite House, had he already given them reason to think that his savage nature was becoming tamed? Did a brighter light burn in the depths of that obscured mind? In short, was the soul returning to the body?

Yes, to a certainty, and to such a degree, that Cyrus Harding and the reporter wondered if the reason of the unfortunate man had ever been totally extinguished. At first, accustomed to the open air, to the unrestrained liberty which he had enjoyed on Tabor Island, the stranger manifested a sullen fury, and it was feared that he might throw himself on to the beach, out of one of the windows of Granite House. But gradually he became calmer, and more freedom was allowed to his movements.

They had reason to hope, and to hope much. Already, forgetting his carnivorous instincts, the stranger accepted a less bestial nourishment than that on which he fed on the islet, and cooked meat did not produce in him the same sentiment of repulsion which he had showed on board the *Bonadventure*. Cyrus Harding had profited by a moment when he was sleeping, to cut his hair and matted beard, which formed a sort of mane, and gave him such a savage aspect. He had also been clothed more suitably, after having got rid of the rag which covered him. The result was that, thanks to these attentions, the stranger resumed a more human appearance, and it even seemed as if his eyes had become milder. Certainly, when formerly lighted up by intelligence, this man's face must have had a sort of beauty.

Every day, Harding imposed on himself the task of passing some hours in his company. He came and worked near him, and occupied himself in different things, so as to fix his attention. A spark, indeed, would be sufficient to reillumine that soul, a recollection crossing that brain to recall reason. That had been seen, during the storm, on board the *Bonadventure!* The engineer did not neglect either to speak aloud, so as to penetrate at the same time by the organs of hearing and sight the depths of that torpid intelligence. Sometimes one of his companions, sometimes another, sometimes all joined him. They spoke most often of things belonging to the navy, which must interest a sailor.

At times the stranger gave some slight attention to what was said, and the settlers were soon convinced that he partly understood them. Sometimes the expression of his countenance was deeply sorrowful, a proof that he suffered mentally, for his face could not be mistaken; but he did not speak, although at different times,

119

however, they almost thought that words were about to issue from his lips. At all events, the poor creature was quite quiet and sad!

But was not his calm only apparent? Was not his sadness only the result of his seclusion? Nothing could yet be ascertained. Seeing only certain objects and in a limited space, always in contact with the colonists, to whom he would soon become accustomed, having no desires to satisfy, better fed, better clothed, it was natural that his physical nature should gradually improve; but was he penetrated with the sense of a new life? or rather, to employ a word, which would be exactly applicable to him, was he not becoming tamed, like an animal in company with his master? This was an important question, which Cyrus Harding was anxious to answer, and yet he did not wish to treat his invalid roughly! would he ever be a convalescent?

How the engineer observed him every moment! How he was on the watch for his soul, if one may use the expression! How he was ready to grasp it! The settlers followed with real sympathy all the phases of the cure undertaken by Harding. They aided him also in this work of humanity, and all, except perhaps the incredulous Pencroft, soon shared both his hope and his faith.

The calm of the stranger was deep, as has been said, and he even showed a sort of attachment for the engineer, whose influence he evidently felt. Cyrus Harding resolved then to try him, by transporting him to another scene, from that ocean which formerly his eyes had been accustomed to contemplate, to the border of the forest, which might perhaps recall those where so many years of his life had been passed!

"But," said Gideon Spilett, "can we hope that he will not escape, if once set at liberty?"

"The experiment must be tried," replied the engineer.

"Well!" said Pencroft. "When that fellow is outside, and feels the fresh air, he will be off as fast as his legs can carry him!"

"I do not think so," returned Harding.

"Let us try," said Spilett.

"We will try," replied the engineer.

This was on the 30th of October, and consequently the castaway of Tabor Island had been a prisoner in Granite House for nine days. It was warm, and a bright sun darted his rays on the island. Cyrus Harding and Pencroft went to the room occupied by the stranger, who was found lying near the window and gazing at the sky.

"Come, my friend," said the engineer to him.

The stranger rose immediately. His eyes were fixed on Cyrus

120

Harding, and he followed him, whilst the sailor marched behind them, little confident as to the result of the experiment.

Arrived at the door, Harding and Pencroft made him take his place in the lift, whilst Neb, Herbert, and Gideon Spilett waited for them before Granite House. The lift descended, and in a few moments all were united on the beach.

The settlers went a short distance from the stranger, so as to leave him at liberty.

He then made a few steps towards the sea, and his look brightened with extreme animation, but he did not make the slightest attempt to escape. He was gazing at the little waves, which broken by the islet rippled on the sand.

"This is only the sea," observed Gideon Spilett, "and possibly it does not inspire him with any wish to escape!"

"Yes," replied Harding, "we must take him to the plateau, on the border of the forest. There the experiment will be more conclusive."

"Besides, he could not run away," said Neb, "since the bridge is raised."

"Oh!" said Pencroft, "that isn't a man to be troubled by a stream like Creek Glycerine! He could cross it directly, at a single bound!"

"We shall soon see," Harding contented himself with replying, his eyes not quitting those of his patient.

The latter was then led towards the mouth of the Mercy, and all climbing the left bank of the river, reached Prospect Heights.

Arrived at the spot on which grew the first beautiful trees of the forest, their foliage slightly agitated by the breeze, the stranger appeared greedily to drink in the penetrating odour which filled the atmosphere, and a long sigh escaped from his chest.

The settlers kept behind him, ready to seize him if he made any movement to escape!

And, indeed, the poor creature was on the point of springing into the creek which separated him from the forest, and his legs were bent for an instant as if for a spring, but almost immediately he stepped back, half sank down, and a large tear fell from his eyes.

"Ah!" exclaimed Cyrus Harding, "you have become a man again, for you can weep!"

CHAPTER XVI

A Mystery to be cleared up—The Stranger's first Words—Twelve Years on the Islet—Avowal which escapes him—The Disappearance—Cyrus Harding's Confidence—Construction of a Mill—The first Bread—An Act of Devotion—Honest Hands.

Yes! the unfortunate man had wept! Some recollection doubtless had flashed across his brain, and to use Cyrus Harding's expression, by those tears he was once more a man.

The colonists left him for some time on the plateau, and withdrew themselves to a short distance, so that he might feel himself free; but he did not think of profiting by this liberty, and Harding soon brought him back to Granite House. Two days after this occurrence, the stranger appeared to wish gradually to mingle with their common life. He evidently heard and understood, but no less evidently was he strangely determined not to speak to the colonists; for one evening, Pencroft, listening at the door of his room, heard these words escape from his lips:—

"No! here! I! never!"

The sailor reported these words to his companions.

"There is some painful mystery there!" said Harding.

The stranger had begun to use the labouring tools, and he worked in the garden. When he stopped in his work, as was often the case, he remained retired within himself; but on the engineer's recommendation, they respected the reserve which he apparently wished to keep. If one of the settlers approached him, he drew back, and his chest heaved with sobs, as if overburthened!

Was it remorse that overwhelmed him thus? They were compelled to believe so, and Gideon Spilett could not help one day making this observation,—

"If he does not speak it is because he has, I fear, things too serious to be told!"

They must be patient and wait.

A few days later, on the 3rd of November, the stranger, working on the plateau, had stopped, letting his spade drop to the ground, and Harding who was observing him from a little distance, saw that tears were again flowing from his eyes. A sort of irresistible pity led him towards the unfortunate man, and he touched his arm lightly.

"My friend!" said he.

The stranger tried to avoid his look, and Cyrus Harding, having endeavoured to take his hand, he drew back quickly.

"My friend," said Harding in a firmer voice, "look at me, I wish it!"

The stranger looked at the engineer, and seemed to be under his power, as a subject under the influence of a mesmerist. He wished to run away. But then his countenance suddenly underwent a transformation. His eyes flashed. Words struggled to escape from his lips. He could no longer contain himself!... At last he folded his arms, then, in a hollow voice,—

"Who are you?" he asked Cyrus Harding.

"Castaways, like you," replied the engineer, whose emotion was deep. "We have brought you here, among your fellow-men."

"My fellow-men!... I have none!"

"You are in the midst of friends."

"Friends!—for me! friends!" exclaimed the stranger, hiding his face in his hands. "No—never—leave me! leave me!"

Then he rushed to the side of the plateau which overlooked the sea, and remained there a long time motionless.

Harding rejoined his companions and related to them what had just happened.

"Yes! there is some mystery in that man's life," said Gideon Spilett, "and it appears as if he had only re-entered society by the path of remorse."

"I don't know what sort of a man we have brought here," said the sailor. "He has secrets—"

"Which we will respect," interrupted Cyrus Harding quickly. "If he has committed any crime, he has most fearfully expiated it, and in our eyes he is absolved."

For two hours the stranger remained alone on the shore, evidently under the influence of recollections which recalled all his past life—a melancholy life doubtless—and the colonists, without losing sight of him, did not attempt to disturb his solitude. However, after two hours, appearing to have formed a resolution, he came to find Cyrus Harding. His eyes were red with the tears he had shed, but he wept no longer. His countenance expressed deep humility. He appeared anxious, timorous, ashamed, and his eyes were constantly fixed on the ground.

"Sir," said he to Harding, "your companions and you, are you English?"

"No," answered the engineer, "we are Americans."

"Ah!" said the stranger, and he murmured, "I prefer that!"

"And you, my friend?" asked the engineer.

123

"English," replied he hastily.

And as if these few words had been difficult to say, he retreated to the beach, where he walked up and down between the cascade and the mouth of the Mercy, in a state of extreme agitation.

Then, passing one moment close to Herbert, he stopped, and in a stifled voice,—

"What month?" he asked.

"December," replied Herbert.

"What year?"

"1866."

"Twelve years! twelve years!" he exclaimed.

Then he left him abruptly.

Herbert reported to the colonists the questions and answers which had been made.

"This unfortunate man," observed Gideon Spilett, "was no longer acquainted with either months or years!"

"Yes!" added Herbert, "and he had been twelve years already on the islet when we found him there!"

"Twelve years!" rejoined Harding. "Ah! twelve years of solitude, after a wicked life, perhaps, may well impair a man's reason!"

"I am induced to think," said Pencroft, "that this man was not wrecked on Tabor Island, but that in consequence of some crime he was left there."

"You must be right, Pencroft," replied the reporter, "and if it is so it is not impossible that those who left him on the island may return to fetch him some day!"

"And they will no longer find him," said Herbert.

"But then," added Pencroft, "they must return, and—"

"My friends," said Cyrus Harding, "do not let us discuss this question until we know more about it. I believe that the unhappy man has suffered, that he has severely expiated his faults, whatever they may have been, and that the wish to unburden himself stifles him. Do not let us press him to tell us his history! He will tell it to us doubtless, and when we know it, we shall see what course it will be best to follow. He alone besides can tell us, if he has more than a hope, a certainty, of returning some day to his country, but I doubt it!"

"And why?" asked the reporter.

"Because that, in the event of his being sure of being delivered at a certain time, he would have waited the hour of his deliverance and would not have thrown this document into the sea. No, it is more probable that he was condemned to die on that islet, and that he never expected to see his fellow-creatures again!"

"But," observed the sailor, "there is one thing which I cannot explain."

"What is it?"

"If this man had been left for twelve years on Tabor Island, one may well suppose that he had been several years already in the wild state in which we found him!"

"That is probable," replied Cyrus Harding.

"It must then be many years since he wrote that document!"

"No doubt, and yet the document appears to have been recently written!"

"Besides, how do you know that the bottle which enclosed the document may not have taken several years to come from Tabor Island to Lincoln Island?"

"That is not absolutely impossible," replied the reporter.

"Might it not have been a long time already on the coast of the island?"

"No," answered Pencroft, "for it was still floating. We could not even suppose that after it had stayed for any length of time on the shore, it would have been swept off by the sea, for the south coast is all rocks, and it would certainly have been smashed to pieces there!"

"That is true," rejoined Cyrus Harding thoughtfully.

"And then," continued the sailor, "if the document was several years old, if it had been shut up in that bottle for several years, it would have been injured by damp. Now, there is nothing of the kind, and it was found in a perfect state of preservation."

The sailor's reasoning was very just, and pointed out an incomprehensible fact, for the document appeared to have been recently written, when the colonists found it in the bottle. Moreover, it gave the latitude and longitude of Tabor Island correctly, which implied that its author had a more complete knowledge of hydrography than could be expected of a common sailor.

"There is in this, again, something unaccountable," said the engineer; "but we will not urge our companion to speak. When he likes, my friends, then we shall be ready to hear him!"

During the following days the stranger did not speak a word, and did not once leave the precincts of the plateau. He worked away, without losing a moment, without taking a minute's rest, but always in a retired place. At meal times he never came to Granite House, although invited several times to do so, but contented himself with eating a few raw vegetables. At nightfall he did not return to the room assigned to him, but remained under some clump of trees, or when the weather was bad crouched in some cleft of the rocks. Thus he lived in the same manner as when he had no other shelter than the forests of Tabor Island, and as all persuasion to induce him to improve his life was in vain, the colonists waited patiently. And the time was near, when, as it seemed, almost involuntarily urged by his conscience, a terrible confession escaped him.

On the 10th of November, about eight o'clock in the evening, as night was coming on, the stranger appeared unexpectedly before the settlers, who were assembled under the verandah. His eyes burned strangely, and he had quite resumed the wild aspect of his worst days.

Cyrus Harding and his companions were astounded on seeing that, overcome by some terrible emotion, his teeth chattered like those of a person in a fever. What was the matter with him? Was the sight of his fellow-creatures insupportable to him? Was he weary of this return to a civilised mode of existence? Was he pining for his former savage life? It appeared so, as soon he was heard to express himself in these incoherent sentences:—

"Why am I here?... By what right have you dragged me from my islet?... Do you think there could be any tie between you and me?... Do you know who I am—what I have done—why I was there—alone? And who told you that I was not abandoned there—that I was not condemned to die there?... Do you know my past?... How do you know that I have not stolen, murdered—that I am not a wretch—an accursed being—only fit to live like a wild beast far from all—speak—do you know it?"

The colonists listened without interrupting the miserable creature, from whom these broken confessions escaped, as it were, in spite of himself. Harding wishing to calm him, approached him, but he hastily drew back.

"No! no!" he exclaimed; "one word only—am I free?"

"You are free," answered the engineer.

"Farewell then!" he cried, and fled like a madman.

Neb, Pencroft, and Herbert ran also towards the edge of the wood—but they returned alone.

"We must let him alone!" said Cyrus Harding.

"He will never come back!" exclaimed Pencroft.

"He will come back," replied the engineer.

Many days passed; but Harding—was it a sort of presentiment?—persisted in the fixed idea that sooner or later the unhappy man would return.

126

"It is the last revolt of his wild nature," said he, "which remorse has touched, and which renewed solitude will terrify."

In the meanwhile, works of all sorts were continued, as well on Prospect Heights as at the corral, where Harding intended to build a farm. It is unnecessary to say that the seeds collected by Herbert on Tabor Island had been carefully sown. The plateau thus formed one immense kitchen-garden, well laid out and carefully tended, so that the arms of the settlers were never in want of work. There was always something to be done. As the esculents increased in number, it became necessary to enlarge the simple beds, which threatened to grow into regular fields and replace the meadows. But grass abounded in other parts of the island, and there was no fear of the onagas being obliged to go on short allowance. It was well worth while, besides, to turn Prospect Heights into a kitchen-garden, defended by its deep belt of creeks, and to remove them to the meadows, which had no need of protection against the depredations of quadrumana and quadrupeds.

On the 15th of November, the third harvest was gathered in. How wonderfully had the field increased in extent, since eighteen months ago, when the first grain of wheat was sown! The second crop of six hundred thousand grains produced this time four thousand bushels, or five hundred millions of grains!

The colony was rich in corn, for ten bushels alone were sufficient for sowing every year to produce an ample crop for the food both of men and beasts. The harvest was completed, and the last fortnight of the month of November was devoted to the work of converting it into food for man. In fact, they had corn, but not flour, and the establishment of a mill was necessary. Cyrus Harding could have utilised the second fall which flowed into the Mercy to establish his motive power, the first being already occupied with moving the felting mill; but after some consultation, it was decided that a simple windmill should be built on Prospect Heights. The building of this presented no more difficulty than the building of the former, and it was moreover certain that there would be no want of wind on the plateau, exposed as it was to the sea breezes.

"Not to mention," said Pencroft, "that the windmill will be more lively and will have a good effect in the landscape!"

They set to work by choosing timber for the frame and machinery of the mill. Some large stones, found at the north of the lake, could be easily transformed into millstones; and as to the sails, the inexhaustible case of the balloon furnished the necessary material.

Cyrus Harding made his model, and the site of the mill was

127

chosen a little to the right of the poultry-yard, near the shore of the lake. The frame was to rest on a pivot supported with strong timbers, so that it could turn with all the machinery it contained according as the wind required it. The work advanced rapidly. Neb and Pencroft had become very skilful carpenters, and had nothing to do but to copy the models provided by the engineer.

Soon a sort of cylindrical box, in shape like a pepperpot, with a pointed roof, rose on the spot chosen. The four frames which formed the sails had been firmly fixed in the centre beam, so as to form a certain angle with it, and secured with iron clamps. As to the different parts of the internal mechanism, the box destined to contain the two millstones, the fixed stone and the moving stone, the hopper, a sort of large square trough, wide at the top, narrow at the bottom, which would allow the grain to fall on the stones, the oscillating spout intended to regulate the passing of the grain, and lastly the bolting machine, which by the operation of sifting, separates the bran from the flour, were made without difficulty. The tools were good, and the work not difficult, for in reality, the machinery of a mill is very simple. This was only a question of time.

Every one had worked at the construction of the mill, and on the 1st of December it was finished. As usual, Pencroft was delighted with his work, and had no doubt that the apparatus was perfect.

"Now for a good wind," said he, "and we shall grind our first harvest splendidly!"

"A good wind, certainly," answered the engineer, "but not too much, Pencroft."

"Pooh! our mill would only go the faster!"

"There is no need for it to go so very fast," replied Cyrus Harding. "It is known by experience that the greatest quantity of work is performed by a mill when the number of turns made by the sails in a minute is six times the number of feet traversed by the wind in a second. A moderate breeze, which passes over twenty-four feet to the second, will give sixteen turns to the sails during a minute, and there is no need of more."

"Exactly!" cried Herbert; "a fine breeze is blowing from the north-east, which will soon do our business for us."

There was no reason for delaying the inauguration of the mill, for the settlers were eager to taste the first piece of bread in Lincoln Island. On this morning two or three bushels of wheat were ground, and the next day at breakfast a magnificent loaf, a little heavy perhaps, although raised with yeast, appeared on the table at Granite House. Every one munched away at it with a pleasure which may be easily understood.

In the meanwhile, the stranger had not reappeared. Several times Gideon Spilett and Herbert searched the forest in the neighbourhood of Granite House, without meeting or finding any trace of him. They became seriously uneasy at this prolonged absence. Certainly, the former savage of Tabor Island could not be perplexed how to live in the forest, abounding in game, but was it not to be feared that he had resumed his habits, and that this freedom would revive in him his wild instincts? However, Harding, by a sort of presentiment, doubtless, always persisted in saying that the fugitive would return.

"Yes, he will return!" he repeated with a confidence which his companions could not share. "When this unfortunate man was on Tabor Island, he knew himself to be alone! Here, he knows that fellow men are awaiting him! Since he has partially spoken of his past life, the poor penitent will return to tell the whole, and from that day he will belong to us!"

The event justified Cyrus Harding's predictions. On the 3rd of December, Herbert had left the plateau to go and fish on the southern bank of the lake. He was unarmed, and till then had never taken any precautions for defence as dangerous animals had not shown themselves on that part of the island.

Meanwhile, Pencroft and Neb were working in the poultry-yard, whilst Harding and the reporter were occupied at the Chimneys in making soda, the store of soap being exhausted.

Suddenly cries resounded,—

"Help! help!"

Cyrus Harding and the reporter, being at too great a distance, had not been able to hear the shouts. Pencroft and Neb, leaving the poultry-yard in all haste, rushed towards the lake.

But before them, the stranger, whose presence at this place no one had suspected, crossed Creek Glycerine, which separated the plateau from the forest, and bounded up the opposite bank.

Herbert was there face to face with a fierce jaguar, similar to the one which had been killed on Reptile End. Suddenly surprised, he was standing with his back against a tree, whilst the animal, gathering itself together, was about to spring.

But the stranger, with no other weapon than a knife, rushed on the formidable animal, who turned to meet this new adversary.

The struggle was short. The stranger possessed immense strength and activity. He seized the jaguar's throat with one powerful hand, holding it as in a vice, without heeding the beast's claws which tore his flesh, and with the other he plunged his knife into its heart.

129

The jaguar fell. The stranger kicked away the body, and was about to fly at the moment when the settlers arrived on the field of battle, but Herbert, clinging to him, cried,—

"No, no! You shall not go!"

Harding advanced towards the stranger, who frowned when he saw him approaching. The blood flowed from his shoulder under his torn shirt, but he took no notice of it.

"My friend," said Cyrus Harding, "we have just contracted a debt of gratitude to you. To save our boy you have risked your life!"

"My life!" murmured the stranger "What is that worth? Less than nothing!"

"You are wounded!"

"It is no matter."

"Will you give me your hand?"

And as Herbert endeavoured to seize the hand which had just saved him, the stranger folded his arms, his chest heaved, his look darkened, and he appeared to wish to escape, but making a violent effort over himself, and in an abrupt tone,—

"Who are you?" he asked, "and what do you claim to be to me?"

It was the colonists' history which he thus demanded, and for the first time. Perhaps this history recounted, he would tell his own.

In a few words Harding related all that had happened since their departure from Richmond; how they had managed, and what resources they now had at their disposal.

The stranger listened with extreme attention.

Then the engineer told who they all were, Gideon Spilett, Herbert, Pencroft, Neb, himself; and he added, that the greatest happiness they had felt since their arrival in Lincoln Island was on the return of the vessel from Tabor Island, when they had been able to include amongst them a new companion.

At these words the stranger's face flushed, his head sunk on his breast, and confusion was depicted on his countenance.

"And now that you know us," added Cyrus Harding, "will you give us your hand?"

"No," replied the stranger in a hoarse voice; "no! You are honest men, you! And I—"

CHAPTER XVII

Still alone—The Stranger's Request—The Farm established at the Corral—Twelve Years ago—The Boatswain's Mate of the *Britannia*— Left on Tabor Island—Cyrus Harding's Hand—The mysterious Document.

These last words justified the colonists' presentiment. There had been some mournful past, perhaps expiated in the sight of men, but from which his conscience had not yet absolved him. At any rate the guilty man felt remorse, he repented, and his new friends would have cordially pressed the hand which they sought; but he did not feel himself worthy to extend it to honest men! However, after the scene with the jaguar, he did not return to the forest, and from that day did not go beyond the enclosure of Granite House.

What was the mystery of his life? Would the stranger one day speak of it? Time alone could show. At any rate, it was agreed that his secret should never be asked from him, and that they would live with him as if they suspected nothing.

For some days their life continued as before. Cyrus Harding and Gideon Spilett worked together, sometimes chemists, sometimes experimentalists. The reporter never left the engineer except to hunt with Herbert, for it would not have been prudent to allow the lad to ramble alone in the forest; and it was very necessary to be on their guard. As to Neb and Pencroft, one day at the stables and poultry-yard, another at the corral, without reckoning work in Granite House, they were never in want of employment.

The stranger worked alone, and he had resumed his usual life, never appearing at meals, sleeping under the trees in the plateau, never mingling with his companions. It really seemed as if the society of those who had saved him was insupportable to him!

"But then," observed Pencroft, "why did he entreat the help of his fellow-creatures? Why did he throw that paper into the sea?"

"He will tell us why," invariably replied Cyrus Harding.

"When?"

"Perhaps sooner than you think, Pencroft."

And, indeed, the day of confession was near.

On the 10th of December, a week after his return to Granite House, Harding saw the stranger approaching, who, in a calm voice and humble tone, said to him: "Sir, I have a request to make you."

"Speak," answered the engineer; "but first let me ask you a question."

At these words the stranger reddened, and was on the point of withdrawing. Cyrus Harding understood what was passing in the mind of the guilty man, who doubtless feared that the engineer would interrogate him on his past life.

Harding held him back.

"Comrade," said he, "we are not only your companions but your friends. I wish you to believe that, and now I will listen to you."

The stranger pressed his hand over his eyes. He was seized with a sort of trembling, and remained a few moments without being able to articulate a word.

"Sir," said he at last, "I have come to beg you to grant me a favour."

"What is it?"

"You have, four or five miles from here, a corral for your domesticated animals. These animals need to be taken care of. Will you allow me to live there with them?"

Cyrus Harding gazed at the unfortunate man for a few moments with a feeling of deep commiseration; then,—

"My friend," said he, "the corral has only stables hardly fit for animals."

"It will be good enough for me, sir."

"My friend," answered Harding, "we will not constrain you in anything. You wish to live at the corral, so be it. You will, however, be always welcome at Granite House. But since you wish to live at the corral we will make the necessary arrangements for your being comfortably established there."

"Never mind that, I shall do very well."

"My friend," answered Harding, who always intentionally made use of this cordial appellation, "you must let us judge what it will be best to do in this respect."

"Thank you, sir," replied the stranger as he withdrew.

The engineer then made known to his companions the proposal which had been made to him, and it was agreed that they should build a wooden house at the corral, which they would make as comfortable as possible.

That very day the colonists repaired to the corral with the necessary tools, and a week had not passed before the house was ready to receive its tenant. It was built about twenty feet from the sheds, and from there it was easy to overlook the flock of sheep, which then numbered more than eighty. Some furniture, a bed, table, bench, cupboard, and chest, were manufactured, and a gun, ammunition, and tools were carried to the corral.

The stranger, however, had seen nothing of his new dwelling, and he had allowed the settlers to work there without him, whilst he occupied himself on the plateau, wishing, doubtless, to put the finishing stroke to his work. Indeed, thanks to him, all the ground was dug up and ready to be sowed when the time came.

It was on the 20th of December that all the arrangements at the corral were completed. The engineer announced to the stranger that his dwelling was ready to receive him, and the latter replied that he would go and sleep there that very evening.

On this evening the colonists were gathered in the dining-room of Granite House. It was then eight o'clock, the hour at which their companion was to leave them. Not wishing to trouble him by their presence, and thus imposing on him the necessity of saying farewells which might perhaps be painful to him, they had left him alone, and ascended to Granite House.

Now, they had been talking in the room for a few minutes, when a light knock was heard at the door. Almost immediately the stranger entered, and without any preamble,—

"Gentlemen," said he, "before I leave you, it is right that you should know my history. I will tell it you."

These simple words profoundly impressed Cyrus Harding and his companions.

The engineer rose.

"We ask you nothing, my friend," said he, "it is your right to be silent."

"It is my duty to speak."

"Sit down, then."

"No, I will stand."

"We are ready to hear you," replied Harding.

The stranger remained standing in a corner of the room, a little in the shade. He was bareheaded, his arms folded across his chest, and it was in this posture that in a hoarse voice, speaking like some one who obliges himself to speak, he gave the following recital, which his auditors did not once interrupt—-

"On the 20th of December, 1854, a steam-yacht, belonging to a Scotch nobleman, Lord Glenarvan, anchored off Cape Bermouilli, on the western coast of Australia, in the thirty-seventh parallel. On board this yacht were Lord Glenarvan and his wife, a major in the English army, a French geographer, a young girl, and a young boy. These two last were the children of Captain Grant, whose ship, the *Britannia*, had been lost, crew and cargo, a year before.

133

The *Duncan* was commanded by Captain John Mangles, and manned by a crew of fifteen men.

"This is the reason the yacht at this time lay off the coast of Australia. Six months before, a bottle, enclosing a document written in English, German, and French, had been found in the Irish sea, and picked up by the *Duncan*. This document stated in substance that there still existed three survivors from the wreck of the *Britannia*, that these survivors were Captain Grant and two of his men, and that they had found refuge on some land, of which the document gave the latitude, but of which the longitude, effaced by the sea, was no longer legible.

"This latitude was 37° 11′ south, therefore, the longitude being unknown, if they followed the thirty-seventh parallel over continents and seas, they would be certain to reach the spot inhabited by Captain Grant and his two companions. The English Admiralty having hesitated to undertake this search, Lord Glenarvan resolved to attempt everything to find the captain. He communicated with Mary and Robert Grant, who joined him. The *Duncan* yacht was equipped for the distant voyage, in which the nobleman's family and the captain's children wished to take part; and the *Duncan*, leaving Glasgow, proceeded towards the Atlantic, passed through the Straits of Magellan, and ascended the Pacific as far as Patagonia, where, according to a previous interpretation of the document, they supposed that Captain Grant was a prisoner among the Indians.

"The *Duncan* disembarked her passengers on the western coast of Patagonia, and sailed to pick them up again on the eastern coast at Cape Corrientes. Lord Glenarvan traversed Patagonia, following the thirty-seventh parallel, and having found no trace of the captain, he re-embarked on the 13th of November, so as to pursue his search through the Ocean.

"After having unsuccessfully visited the islands of Tristan d'Acunha and Amsterdam, situated in her course, the *Duncan*, as I have said, arrived at Cape Bermouilli, on the Australian coast, on the 20th of December, 1854.

"It was Lord Glenarvan's intention to traverse Australia as he had traversed America, and he disembarked. A few miles from the coast was established a farm, belonging to an Irishman, who offered hospitality to the travellers. Lord Glenarvan made known to the Irishman the cause which had brought him to these parts, and asked if he knew whether a three-masted English vessel, the *Britannia*, had been lost less than two years before on the west coast of Australia.

"The Irishman had never heard of this wreck; but, to the great surprise of the bystanders, one of his servants came forward and said,—

"'My lord, praise and thank God! If Captain Grant is still living, he is living on the Australian shores.'

"'Who are you?' asked Lord Glenarvan.

"'A Scotchman like yourself, my lord,' replied the man; 'I am one of Captain Grant's crew—one of the castaways of the *Britannia*.'

"This man was called Ayrton. He was, in fact, the boatswain's mate of the *Britannia*, as his papers showed. But, separated from Captain Grant at the moment when the ship struck upon the rocks, he had till then believed that the captain with all his crew had perished, and that he, Ayrton, was the sole survivor of the *Britannia*.

"'Only,' added he, 'it was not on the west coast, but on the east coast of Australia that the vessel was lost; and if Captain Grant is still living, as his document indicates, he is a prisoner among the natives, and it is on the other coast that he must be looked for.'

"This man spoke in a frank voice and with a confident look; his words could not be doubted. The Irishman, in whose service he had been for more than a year, answered for his trustworthiness. Lord Glenarvan, therefore, believed in the fidelity of this man, and, by his advice, resolved to cross Australia, following the thirty-seventh parallel. Lord Glenarvan, his wife, the two children, the major, the Frenchman, Captain Mangles, and a few sailors composed the little band under the command of Ayrton, whilst the *Duncan*, under charge of the mate, Tom Austin, proceeded to Melbourne, there to await Lord Glenarvan's instructions.

"They set out on the 23rd of December, 1854.

"It is time to say that Ayrton was a traitor. He was, indeed, the boatswain's mate of the *Britannia*; but, after some dispute with his captain, he had endeavoured to incite the crew to mutiny and seize the ship, and Captain Grant had landed him, on the 8th of April, 1852, on the west coast of Australia, and then sailed, leaving him there, as was only just.

"Therefore this wretched man knew nothing of the wreck of the *Britannia*; he had just heard of it from Glenarvan's account. Since his abandonment, he had become, under the name of Ben Joyce, the leader of the escaped convicts; and if he boldly maintained that the wreck had taken place on the east coast, and led Lord Glenarvan to proceed in that direction, it was that he hoped to separate him from his ship, seize the *Duncan*, and make the yacht a pirate in the Pacific."

135

Here the stranger stopped for a moment. His voice trembled, but he continued,—

"The expedition set out and proceeded across Australia. It was inevitably unfortunate, since Ayrton, or Ben Joyce, as he may be called, guided it, sometimes preceded, sometimes followed by his band of convicts, who had been told what they had to do.

"Meanwhile the *Duncan* had been sent to Melbourne for repairs. It was necessary, then, to get Lord Glenarvan to order her to leave Melbourne and go to the east coast of Australia, where it would be easy to seize her. After having led the expedition near enough to the coast, in the midst of vast forests with no resources, Ayrton obtained a letter, which he was charged to carry to the mate of the *Duncan*—a letter which ordered the yacht to repair immediately to the east coast, to Twofold Bay, that is to say, a few days' journey from the place where the expedition had stopped. It was there that Ayrton had agreed to meet his accomplices, and two days after gaining possession of the letter, he arrived at Melbourne.

"So far the villain had succeeded in his wicked design. He would be able to take the *Duncan* into Twofold Bay, where it would be easy for the convicts to seize her, and her crew massacred, Ben Joyce would become master of the seas.... But it pleased God to prevent the accomplishment of these terrible projects.

"Ayrton, arrived at Melbourne, delivered the letter to the mate, Tom Austin, who read it and immediately set sail; but judge of Ayrton's rage and disappointment, when the next day he found that the mate was taking the vessel, not to the east coast of Australia, to Twofold Bay, but to the east coast of New Zealand. He wished to stop him, but Austin showed him the letter!... And indeed, by a providential error of the French geographer, who had written the letter, the east coast of New Zealand was mentioned as the place of destination.

"All Ayrton's plans were frustrated! He became outrageous. They put him in irons. He was then taken to the coast of New Zealand, not knowing what would become of his accomplices, or what would become of Lord Glenarvan.

"The *Duncan* cruised about on this coast until the 3rd of March. On that day Ayrton heard the report of guns. The guns of the *Duncan* were being fired, and soon Lord Glenarvan and his companions came on board.

"This is what had happened.

"After a thousand hardships, a thousand dangers, Lord Glenarvan had accomplished his journey, and arrived on the east coast of Australia, at Twofold Bay. 'No *Duncan!*' he telegraphed to

Melbourne. They answered, '*Duncan* sailed on the 18th instant. Destination unknown.'

"Lord Glenarvan could only arrive at one conclusion: that his honest yacht had fallen into the hands of Ben Joyce, and had become a pirate vessel!

"However, Lord Glenarvan would not give up. He was a bold and generous man. He embarked in a merchant vessel, sailed to the west coast of New Zealand, traversed it along the thirty-seventh parallel, without finding any trace of Captain Grant; but on the other side, to his great surprise, and by the will of Heaven, he found the *Duncan,* under command of the mate, who had been waiting for him for five weeks!

"This was on the 3rd of March 1855. Lord Glenarvan was now on board the *Duncan,* but Ayrton was there also. He appeared before the nobleman, who wished to extract from him all that the villain knew about Captain Grant. Ayrton refused to speak. Lord Glenarvan then told him, that at the first port they put into, he would be delivered up to the English authorities. Ayrton remained mute.

"The *Duncan* continued her voyage along the thirty-seventh parallel. In the meanwhile, Lady Glenarvan undertook to vanquish the resistance of the ruffian.

"At last, her influence prevailed, and Ayrton, in exchange for what he could tell, proposed that Lord Glenarvan should leave him on some island in the Pacific, instead of giving him up to the English authorities. Lord Glenarvan, resolving to do anything to obtain information about Captain Grant, consented.

"Ayrton then related all his life, and it was certain that he knew nothing from the day on which Captain Grant had landed him on the Australian coast.

"Nevertheless, Lord Glenarvan kept the promise which he had given. The *Duncan* continued her voyage and arrived at Tabor Island. It was there that Ayrton was to be landed, and it was there also that, by a veritable miracle, they found Captain Grant and two men, exactly on the thirty-seventh parallel.

"The convict, then, went to take their place on this desert islet, and at the moment he left the yacht these words were pronounced by Lord Glenarvan:—

"'Here, Ayrton, you will be far from any land, and without any possible communication with your fellow-creatures. You cannot escape from this islet on which the *Duncan* leaves you. You will be alone, under the eye of a God who reads the depths of the heart; but you will be neither lost nor forgotten, as was Captain Grant.

137

Unworthy as you are to be remembered by men, men will remember you. I know where you are, Ayrton, and I know where to find you. I will never forget it!'

"And the *Duncan*, making sail, soon disappeared. This was on the 18th of March 1855. [2]

"Ayrton was alone, but he had no want of either ammunition, weapons, tools, or seeds.

"At his, the convict's disposal, was the house built by honest Captain Grant. He had only to live and expiate in solitude the crimes which he had committed.

"Gentlemen, he repented, he was ashamed of his crimes and was very miserable! He said to himself, that if men came some day to take him from that islet, he must be worthy to return amongst them! How he suffered, that wretched man! How he laboured to recover himself by work! How he prayed to be reformed by prayer! For two years, three years, this went on; but Ayrton, humbled by solitude, always looking for some ship to appear on the horizon, asking himself if the time of expiation would soon be complete, suffered as none other ever suffered! Oh! how dreadful was this solitude, to a heart tormented by remorse!

"But doubtless Heaven had not sufficiently punished this unhappy man, for he felt that he was gradually becoming a savage! He felt that brutishness was gradually gaining on him!

"He could not say if it was after two or three years of solitude; but at last he became the miserable creature you found!

"I have no need to tell you, gentlemen, that Ayrton, Ben Joyce, and I, are the same."

Cyrus Harding and his companions rose at the end of this account. It is impossible to say how much they were moved! What misery, grief, and despair lay revealed before them!

"Ayrton," said Harding, rising, "you have been a great criminal, but Heaven must certainly think that you have expiated your crimes! That has been proved by your having been brought again among your fellow-creatures. Ayrton, you are forgiven! And now you will be our companion?"

Ayrton drew back.

"Here is my hand!" said the engineer.

---

[2] The events which have just been briefly related are taken from a work which some of our readers have no doubt read, and which is entitled Captain Grant's Children. They will remark on this occasion, as well as later, some discrepancy in the dates: but later again, they will understand why the real dates were not at first given.

Ayrton grasped the hand which Harding extended to him, and great tears fell from his eyes.

"Will you live with us?" asked Cyrus Harding.

"Captain Harding, leave me some time longer," replied Ayrton, "leave me alone in the hut in the corral!"

"As you like, Ayrton," answered Cyrus Harding. Ayrton was going to withdraw, when the engineer addressed one more question to him:—

"One word more, my friend. Since it was your intention to live alone, why did you throw into the sea the document which put us on your track?"

"A document?" repeated Ayrton, who did not appear to know what he meant.

"Yes, the document which we found enclosed in a bottle, giving us the exact position of Tabor Island!"

Ayrton passed his hand over his brow, then after having thought, "I never threw any document into the sea!" he answered.

"Never," exclaimed Pencroft.

"Never!"

And Ayrton, bowing, reached the door and departed.

CHAPTER XVIII

Conversation—Cyrus Harding and Gideon Spilett—
An Idea of the Engineer's—The Electric Telegraph—The
Wires—The Battery—The Alphabet—Fine Season—
Prosperity of the Colony—Photography—An Appearance of
Snow—Two Years in Lincoln Island.

"Poor man!" said Herbert, who had rushed to the door, but returned, having seen Ayrton slide down the rope of the lift and disappear in the darkness.

"He will come back," said Cyrus Harding.

"Come now, captain," exclaimed Pencroft, "what does that mean? What! wasn't it Ayrton who threw that bottle into the sea? Who was it then?"

Certainly, if ever a question was necessary to be made, it was that one!

"It was he," answered Neb, "only the unhappy man was half mad."

"Yes!" said Herbert, "and he was no longer conscious of what he was doing."

"It can only be explained in that way, my friends," replied Harding quickly, "and I understand now how Ayrton was able to point out exactly the situation of Tabor Island, since the events which had preceded his being left on the Island had made it known to him."

"However," observed Pencroft, "if he was not yet a brute when he wrote that document, and if he threw it into the sea seven or eight years ago, how is it that the paper has not been injured by damp?"

"That proves," answered Cyrus Harding, "that Ayrton was deprived of intelligence at a more recent time than he thinks."

"Of course it must be so," replied Pencroft, "without that the fact would be unaccountable."

"Unaccountable indeed," answered the engineer, who did not appear desirous to prolong the conversation.

"But has Ayrton told the truth?" asked the sailor.

"Yes," replied the reporter. "The story which he has told is true in every point. I remember quite well the account in the newspapers of the yacht expedition undertaken by Lord Glenarvan, and its result."

"Ayrton has told the truth," added Harding. "Do not doubt it,

Pencroft, for it was painful to him. People tell the truth when they accuse themselves like that!"

The next day—the 21st of December—the colonists descended to the beach, and having climbed the plateau they found nothing of Ayrton. He had reached his house in the corral during the night, and the settlers judged it best not to agitate him by their presence. Time would doubtless perform what sympathy had been unable to accomplish.

Herbert, Pencroft, and Neb resumed their ordinary occupations. On this day the same work brought Harding and the reporter to the workshop at the Chimneys.

"Do you know, my dear Cyrus," said Gideon Spilett, "that the explanation you gave yesterday on the subject of the bottle has not satisfied me at all! How can it be supposed that the unfortunate man was able to write that document and throw the bottle into the sea without having the slightest recollection of it?"

"Nor was it he who threw it in, my dear Spilett."

"You think then...."

"I think nothing, I know nothing!" interrupted Cyrus Harding. "I am content to rank this incident among those which I have not been able to explain to this day!"

"Indeed, Cyrus," said Spilett, "these things are incredible! Your rescue, the case stranded on the sand, Top's adventure, and lastly this bottle.... Shall we never have the answer to these enigmas?"

"Yes!" replied the engineer quickly, "yes, even if I have to penetrate into the bowels of this island!"

"Chance will perhaps give us the key to this mystery!"

"Chance! Spilett! I do not believe in chance, any more than I believe in mysteries in this world. There is a reason for everything unaccountable which has happened here, and that reason I shall discover. But in the meantime we must work and observe."

The month of January arrived. The year 1867 commenced. The summer occupations were assiduously continued. During the days which followed, Herbert and Spilett having gone in the direction of the corral, ascertained that Ayrton had taken possession of the habitation which had been prepared for him. He busied himself with the numerous flock confided to his care, and spared his companions the trouble of coming every two or three days to visit the corral. Nevertheless, in order not to leave Ayrton in solitude for too long a time, the settlers often paid him a visit.

It was not unimportant either, in consequence of some suspicions entertained by the engineer and Gideon Spilett, that this part of the island should be subject to a surveillance of some sort, and that Ayrton, if any incident occurred unexpectedly, should not neglect to inform the inhabitants of Granite House of it.

Nevertheless it might happen that something would occur which it would be necessary to bring rapidly to the engineer's knowledge. Independently of facts bearing on the mystery of Lincoln Island, many others might happen, which would call for the prompt interference of the colonists,—such as the sighting of a vessel, a wreck on the western coast, the possible arrival of pirates, etc.

Therefore Cyrus Harding resolved to put the corral in instantaneous communication with Granite House.

It was on the 10th of January that he made known his project to his companions.

"Why! how are you going to manage that, captain?" asked Pencroft. "Do you by chance happen to think of establishing a telegraph?"

"Exactly so," answered the engineer.

"Electric?" cried Herbert.

"Electric," replied Cyrus Harding. "We have all the necessary materials for making a battery, and the most difficult thing will be to stretch the wires, but by means of a draw-plate I think we shall manage it."

"Well, after that," returned the sailor, "I shall never despair of seeing ourselves some day rolling along on a railway!"

They then set to work, beginning with the most difficult thing, for, if they failed in that, it would be useless to manufacture the battery and other accessories.

The iron of Lincoln Island, as has been said, was of excellent quality, and consequently very fit for being drawn out. Harding commenced by manufacturing a draw-plate, that is to say, a plate of steel, pierced with conical holes of different sizes, which would successively bring the wire to the wished-for tenacity. This piece of steel, after having been tempered, was fixed in as firm a way as possible in a solid framework planted in the ground, only a few feet from the great fall, the motive power of which the engineer intended to utilise. In fact, as the fulling-mill was there, although not then in use, its beam moved with extreme power would serve to stretch out the wire by rolling it round itself. It was a delicate operation, and required much care. The iron, prepared previously in long thin rods, the ends of which were sharpened with the file, having been introduced into the largest hole of the draw-plate, was drawn out by the beam which wound it round itself, to a length of twenty-five or thirty feet, then unrolled, and the same operation was performed successively through the holes of a less size. Finally, the engineer obtained wires from forty to fifty feet long, which could be easily fastened together and stretched over the distance of five miles, which separated the corral from the bounds of Granite House.

It did not take more than a few days to perform this work, and indeed as soon as the machine had been commenced, Cyrus Harding left his companions to follow the trade of wire-drawers, and occupied himself with manufacturing his battery.

It was necessary to obtain a battery with a constant current. It is known that the elements of modern batteries are generally composed of retort coal, zinc, and copper. Copper was absolutely wanting to the engineer, who, notwithstanding all his researches, had never been able to find any trace of it in Lincoln Island, and was therefore obliged to do without it. Retort coal, that is to say, the hard graphyte which is found in the retorts of gas manufactories, after the coal has been dehydrogenised, could have been obtained, but it would have been necessary to establish a special apparatus, involving great labour. As to zinc, it may be remembered that the case found at Flotsam Point was lined with this metal, which could not be better utilised than for this purpose.

Cyrus Harding, after mature consideration, decided to manufacture a very simple battery, resembling as nearly as possible that invented by Becquerel in 1820, and in which zinc only is employed. The other substances, azotic acid and potash, were all at his disposal.

The way in which the battery was composed was as follows, and the results were to be attained by the reaction of acid and potash on each other. A number of glass bottles were made and filled with azotic acid. The engineer corked them by means of a stopper through which passed a glass tube, bored at its lower extremity, and intended to be plunged into the acid by means of a clay stopper secured by a rag. Into this tube, through its upper extremity, he poured a solution of potash, previously obtained by burning and reducing to ashes various plants, and in this way the acid and potash could act on each other through the clay.

Cyrus Harding then took two slips of zinc, one of which was plunged into azotic acid, the other into a solution of potash. A current was immediately produced, which was transmitted from the slip of zinc in the bottle to that in the tube, and the two slips having been connected by a metallic wire the slip in the tube became the positive pole, and that in the bottle the negative pole of the apparatus. Each bottle, therefore, produced as many currents as united would be sufficient to produce all the phenomena of the electric telegraph. Such was the ingenious and very simple apparatus constructed by Cyrus Harding, an apparatus which would allow them to establish a telegraphic communication between Granite House and the corral.

On the 6th of February was commenced the planting, along the road to the corral, of posts, furnished with glass insulators, and intended to support the wire. A few days after, the wire was extended, ready to produce the electric current at a rate of twenty thousand miles a second.

Two batteries had been manufactured, one for Granite House, the other for the corral; for if it was necessary the corral should be able to communicate with Granite House, it might also be useful that Granite House should be able to communicate with the corral.

As to the receiver and manipulator, they were very simple. At the two stations the wire was wound round a magnet, that is to say, round a piece of soft iron surrounded with a wire. The communication was thus established between the two poles, the current, starting from the positive pole, traversed the wire, passed through the magnet which was temporarily magnetised, and returned through the earth to the negative pole. If the current was interrupted the magnet immediately became unmagnetised. It was sufficient to place a plate of soft iron before the magnet, which, attracted during the passage of the current, would fall back when the current was interrupted. This movement of the plate thus obtained, Harding could easily fasten to it a needle arranged on a dial, bearing the letters of the alphabet, and in this way communicate from one station to the other.

All was completely arranged by the 12th of February. On this day, Harding, having sent the current through the wire, asked if all was going on well at the corral, and received in a few moments a satisfactory reply from Ayrton. Pencroft was wild with joy, and every morning and evening he sent a telegram to the corral, which always received an answer.

This mode of communication presented two very real advantages; firstly, because it enabled them to ascertain that Ayrton was at the corral, and secondly, that he was thus not left completely isolated. Besides, Cyrus Harding never allowed a week to pass without going to see him, and Ayrton came from time to time to Granite House, where he always found a cordial welcome.

The fine season passed away in the midst of the usual work. The resources of the colony, particularly in vegetables and corn, increased from day to day; and the plants brought from Tabor Island had succeeded perfectly.

The plateau of Prospect Heights presented an encouraging aspect. The fourth harvest had been admirable, and it may be supposed that no one thought of counting whether the four hundred thousand millions of grains duly appeared in the crop. However, Pencroft had thought of doing so, but Cyrus Harding having told him that even if he managed to count three hundred grains a minute, or nine thousand an hour, it would take him nearly five thousand five hundred years to finish his task, the honest sailor considered it best to give up the idea.

The weather was splendid, the temperature very warm in the day time; but in the evening the sea-breezes tempered the heat of the atmosphere and procured cool nights for the inhabitants of Granite House. There were, however, a few storms, which, although they were not of long duration, swept over Lincoln Island with extraordinary fury. The lightning blazed and the thunder continued to roll for some hours.

At this period the little colony was extremely prosperous.

The tenants of the poultry-yard swarmed, and they lived on the surplus, but it became necessary to reduce the population to a more moderate number. The pigs had already produced young, and it may be understood that their care for those animals absorbed a great part of Neb and Pencroft's time. The onagas, who had two pretty colts, were most often mounted by Gideon Spilett and Herbert, who had become an excellent rider under the reporter's instruction, and they also harnessed them to the cart either for carrying wood and coal to Granite House, or different mineral productions required by the engineer.

Several expeditions were made about this time into the depths of the Far West Forests. The explorers could venture there without having anything to fear from the heat, for the sun's rays scarcely penetrated through the thick foliage spreading above their heads. They thus visited all the left bank of the Mercy, along which ran the road from the corral to the mouth of Falls River.

But in these excursions the settlers took care to be well armed, for they frequently met with savage wild boars, with which they often had a tussle. They also, during this season, made fierce war against the jaguars. Gideon Spilett had vowed a special hatred against them, and his pupil Herbert seconded him well. Armed as they were, they no longer feared to meet one of those beasts. Herbert's courage was superb, and the reporter's *sang froid* astonishing. Already twenty magnificent skins ornamented the dining-room of Granite House, and if this continued, the jaguar race would soon be extinct in the island, the object aimed at by the hunters.

The engineer sometimes took part in the expeditions made to the unknown parts of the island, which he surveyed with great attention. It was for other traces than those of animals that he searched the thickest of the vast forest, but nothing suspicious ever appeared. Neither Top nor Jup, who accompanied him, ever betrayed by their behaviour that there was anything strange there, and yet more than once again the dog barked at the mouth of the well, which the engineer had before explored without result.

At this time Gideon Spilett, aided by Herbert, took several views of the most picturesque parts of the island, by means of the photographic apparatus found in the cases, and of which they had not as yet made any use.

This apparatus, provided with a powerful object-glass, was very complete. Substances necessary for the photographic reproduction, collodion for preparing the glass plate, nitrate of silver to render it sensitive, hyposulphate of soda to fix the prints obtained, chloride of ammonium in which to soak the paper destined to give the positive proof, acetate of soda and chloride of gold in which to immerse the paper, nothing was wanting. Even the papers were there, all prepared, and before laying in the printing-frame upon the negatives, it was sufficient to soak them for a few minutes in the solution of nitrate of silver.

The reporter and his assistant became in a short time very skilful operators, and they obtained fine views of the country, such as the island, taken from Prospect Heights with Mount Franklin in the distance, the mouth of the Mercy, so picturesquely framed in high rocks, the glade and the corral, with the spurs of the mountain in the background, the curious development of Claw Cape, Flotsam Point, etc.

Nor did the photographers forget to take the portraits of all the inhabitants of the island, leaving out no one.

"It multiplies us," said Pencroft.

And the sailor was enchanted to see his own countenance, faithfully reproduced, ornamenting the walls of Granite House, and he stopped as willingly before this exhibition as he would have done before the richest shop-windows in Broadway.

But it must be acknowledged that the most successful portrait was incontestably that of Master Jup. Master Jup had sat with a gravity not to be described, and his portrait was lifelike!

"He looks as if he was just going to grin!" exclaimed Pencroft.

And if Master Jup had not been satisfied, he would have been very difficult to please, but he was quite contented, and contemplated his own countenance with a sentimental air which expressed some small amount of conceit.

The summer heat ended with the month of March. The weather was sometimes rainy, but still warm. The month of March, which corresponds to the September of northern latitudes, was not so fine as might have been hoped. Perhaps it announced an early and rigorous winter.

It might have been supposed one morning—the 21st—that the first snow had already made its appearance. In fact Herbert, looking early from one of the windows of Granite House, exclaimed,—

"Hallo! the islet is covered with snow!"

"Snow at this time?" answered the reporter, joining the boy.

Their companions were soon beside them, but could only ascertain one thing, that not only the islet, but all the beach below Granite House, was covered with one uniform sheet of white.

"It must be snow!" said Pencroft.

"Or rather it's very like it!" replied Neb.

"But the thermometer marks fifty-eight degrees!" observed Gideon Spilett.

Cyrus Harding gazed at the sheet of white without saying anything, for he really did not know how to explain this phenomenon, at this time of year and in such a temperature.

"By Jove!" exclaimed Pencroft, "all our plants will be frozen!"

And the sailor was about to descend, when he was preceded by the nimble Jup, who slid down to the sand.

But the orang had not touched the ground, when the snowy sheet arose and dispersed in the air in such innumerable flakes that the light of the sun was obscured for some minutes.

"Birds!" cried Herbert.

They were indeed swarms of sea-birds, with dazzling white plumage. They had perched by thousands on the islet and on the shore, and they disappeared in the distance, leaving the colonists amazed as if they had been present at some transformation scene, in which summer succeeded winter at the touch of a fairy's wand. Unfortunately the change had been so sudden that neither the reporter nor the lad had been able to bring down one of these birds, of which they could not recognise the species.

A few days after came the 26th of March, the day on which, two years before, the castaways from the air had been thrown upon Lincoln Island.

CHAPTER XIX

Recollections of their Native Land—Probable Future—Project for surveying the Coasts of the Island— Departure on the 16th of April—Sea-view of Reptile End— The basaltic Rocks of the Western Coast—Bad Weather— Night comes on—New Incident.

Two years already! and for two years the colonists had had no communication with their fellow-creatures! They were without news from the civilised world, lost on this island, as completely as if they had been on the most minute star of the celestial hemisphere!

What was now happening in their country? The picture of their native land was always before their eyes, the land torn by civil war at the time they left it, and which the Southern rebellion was perhaps still staining with blood! It was a great sorrow to them, and they often talked together of these things, without ever doubting however that the cause of the North must triumph, for the honour of the American Confederation.

During these two years not a vessel had passed in sight of the island; or, at least, not a sail had been seen. It was evident that Lincoln Island was out of the usual track, and also that it was unknown,—as was besides proved by the maps,—for though there was no port, vessels might have visited it for the purpose of renewing their store of water. But the surrounding ocean was deserted as far as the eye could reach, and the colonists must rely on themselves for regaining their native land.

However, one chance of rescue existed, and this chance was discussed one day in the first week of April, when the colonists were gathered together in the dining-room of Granite House.

They had been talking of America, of their native country, which they had so little hope of ever seeing again.

"Decidedly we have only one way," said Spilett, "one single way for leaving Lincoln Island, and that is, to build a vessel large enough to sail several hundred miles. It appears to me, that when one has built a boat it is just as easy to build a ship!"

"And in which we might go to the Pomatous," added Herbert, "just as easily as we went to Tabor Island."

"I do not say no," replied Pencroft, who had always the casting vote in maritime questions; "I do not say no, although it is not exactly the same thing to make a long as a short voyage! If our little craft had been caught in any heavy gale of wind during the voyage to

Tabor Island, we should have known that land was at no great distance either way; but twelve hundred miles is a pretty long way, and the nearest land is at least that distance!"

"Would you not, in that case, Pencroft, attempt the adventure?" asked the reporter.

"I will attempt anything that is desired, Mr. Spilett," answered the sailor, "and you know well that I am not a man to flinch!"

"Remember, besides, that we number another sailor amongst us now," remarked Neb.

"Who is that?" asked Pencroft.

"Ayrton."

"That is true," replied Herbert.

"If he will consent to come," said Pencroft.

"Nonsense!" returned the reporter; "do you think that if Lord Glenarvan's yacht had appeared at Tabor Island, whilst he was still living there, Ayrton would have refused to depart?"

"You forget, my friends," then said Cyrus Harding, "that Ayrton was not in possession of his reason during the last years of his stay there. But that is not the question. The point is to know if we may count among our chances of being rescued, the return of the Scotch vessel. Now, Lord Glenarvan promised Ayrton that he would return to take him off Tabor Island when he considered that his crimes were expiated, and I believe that he will return."

"Yes," said the reporter, "and I will add that he will return soon, for it is twelve years since Ayrton was abandoned!"

"Well!" answered Pencroft, "I agree with you that the nobleman will return, and soon too. But where will he touch? At Tabor Island, and not at Lincoln Island."

"That is the more certain," replied Herbert, "as Lincoln Island is not even marked on the map."

"Therefore, my friends," said the engineer, "we ought to take the necessary precautions for making our presence, and that of Ayrton on Lincoln Island known at Tabor Island."

"Certainly," answered the reporter, "and nothing is easier than to place in the hut, which was Captain Grant's and Ayrton's dwelling, a notice which Lord Glenarvan and his crew cannot help finding, giving the position of our island."

"It is a pity," remarked the sailor, "that we forgot to take that precaution on our first visit to Tabor Island."

"And why should we have done it?" asked Herbert.

"At that time we did not know Ayrton's history; we did not know that any one was likely to come some day to fetch him; and

149

when we did know his history, the season was too advanced to allow us to return then to Tabor Island."

"Yes," replied Harding, "it was too late, and we must put off the voyage until next spring."

"But suppose the Scotch yacht comes before that," said Pencroft.

"That is not probable," replied the engineer, "for Lord Glenarvan would not choose the winter season to venture into these seas. Either he has already returned to Tabor Island, since Ayrton has been with us, that is to say, during the last five months and has left again; or he will not come till later, and it will be time enough in the first fine October days to go to Tabor Island, and leave a notice there."

"We must allow," said Neb, "that it will be very unfortunate if the *Duncan* has returned to these parts only a few months ago!"

"I hope that it is not so," replied Cyrus Harding, "and that Heaven has not deprived us of the best chance which remains to us."

"I think," observed the reporter, "that at any rate we shall know what we have to depend on when we have been to Tabor Island, for if the yacht has returned there, they will necessarily have left some traces of their visit."

"That is evident," answered the engineer. "So then, my friends, since we have this chance of returning to our country, we must wait patiently, and if it is taken from us we shall see what will be best to do."

"At any rate," remarked Pencroft, "it is well understood that if we do leave Lincoln Island in some way or another, it will not be because we were uncomfortable there!"

"No, Pencroft," replied the engineer, "it will be because we are far from all that a man holds dearest in this world, his family, his friends, his native land!"

Matters being thus decided, the building of a vessel large enough to sail either to the Archipelagos in the north, or to New Zealand in the west, was no longer talked of, and they busied themselves in their accustomed occupations, with a view to wintering a third time in Granite House.

However, it was agreed that before the stormy weather came on, their little vessel should be employed in making a voyage round the island. A complete survey of the coast had not yet been made, and the colonists had but an imperfect idea of the shore to the west and north, from the mouth of Falls River to the Mandible Capes, as well as of the narrow bay between them, which opened like a shark's jaws.

The plan of this excursion was proposed by Pencroft, and Cyrus Harding fully acquiesced in it, for he himself wished to see this part of his domain.

The weather was variable, but the barometer did not fluctuate by sudden movements, and they could therefore count on tolerable weather. However, during the first week of April, after a sudden barometrical fall, a renewed rise was marked by a heavy gale of wind, lasting five or six days; then the needle of the instrument remained stationary at a height of twenty-nine inches and nine-tenths, and the weather appeared propitious for an excursion.

The departure was fixed for the 16th of April, and the *Bonadventure*, anchored in Port Balloon, was provisioned for a voyage which might be of some duration.

Cyrus Harding informed Ayrton of the projected expedition, and proposed that he should take part in it; but Ayrton preferring to remain on shore, it was decided that he should come to Granite House during the absence of his companions. Master Jup was ordered to keep him company, and made no remonstrance.

On the morning of the 16th of April all the colonists, including Top, embarked. A fine breeze blew from the south-west, and the *Bonadventure* tacked on leaving Port Balloon so as to reach Reptile End. Of the ninety miles which the perimeter of the island measured, twenty included the south coast between the port and the promontory. The wind being right ahead, it was necessary to hug the shore.

It took the whole day to reach the promontory, for the vessel on leaving port had only two hours of the ebb tide, and had therefore to make way for six hours against the flood. It was nightfall before the promontory was doubled.

The sailor then proposed to the engineer that they should continue sailing slowly with two reefs in the sail. But Harding preferred to anchor a few cable-lengths from the shore, so as to survey that part of the coast during the day. It was agreed also that as they were anxious for a minute exploration of the coast they should not sail during the night, but would always, when the weather permitted it, be at anchor near the shore.

The night was passed under the promontory, and the wind having fallen, nothing disturbed the silence. The passengers, with the exception of the sailor, scarcely slept as well on board the *Bonadventure* as they would have done in their rooms at Granite House, but they did sleep however. Pencroft set sail at break of day, and by going on the larboard tack they could keep close to the shore.

The colonists knew this beautiful wooded coast, since they had already explored it on foot, and yet it again excited their admiration. They coasted along as close in as possible, so as to notice everything, avoiding always the trunks of trees which floated here and there. Several times also they anchored, and Gideon Spilett took photographs of the superb scenery.

About noon the *Bonadventure* arrived at the mouth of Falls River. Beyond, on the left bank, a few scattered trees appeared, and three miles further even these dwindled into solitary groups among the western spurs of the mountain, whose arid ridge sloped down to the shore.

What a contrast between the northern and southern part of the coast! In proportion as one was woody and fertile so was the other rugged and barren! It might have been designated as one of those iron coasts, as they are called in some countries, and its wild confusion appeared to indicate that a sudden crystallisation had been produced in the yet liquid basalt of some distant geological sea. These stupendous masses would have terrified the settlers if they had been cast at first on this part of the island! They had not been able to perceive the sinister aspect of this shore from the summit of Mount Franklin, for they overlooked it from too great a height, but viewed from the sea it presented a wild appearance which could not perhaps be equalled in any corner of the globe.

The *Bonadventure* sailed along this coast for the distance of half a mile. It was easy to see that it was composed of blocks of all sizes, from twenty to three hundred feet in height, and of all shapes, round like towers, prismatic like steeples, pyramidal like obelisks, conical like factory chimneys. An iceberg of the Polar seas could not have been more capricious in its terrible sublimity! Here, bridges were thrown from one rock to another; there, arches like those of a wave, into the depths of which the eye could not penetrate; in one place, large vaulted excavations presented a monumental aspect; in another, a crowd of columns, spires, and arches, such as no Gothic cathedral ever possessed. Every caprice of nature, still more varied than those of the imagination, appeared on this grand coast, which extended over a length of eight or nine miles.

Cyrus Harding and his companions gazed, with a feeling of surprise bordering on stupefaction. But, although they remained silent, Top, not being troubled with feelings of this sort, uttered barks which were repeated by the thousand echoes of the basaltic cliff. The engineer even observed that these barks had something

152

strange in them, like those which the dog had uttered at the mouth of the well in Granite House.

"Let us go close in," said he.

And the *Bonadventure* sailed as near as possible to the rocky shore. Perhaps some cave, which it would be advisable to explore, existed there? But Harding saw nothing, not a cavern, not a cleft which could serve as a retreat to any being whatever, for the foot of the cliff was washed by the surf. Soon Top's barks ceased, and the vessel continued her course at a few cable-lengths from the coast.

In the north-west part of the island the shore became again flat and sandy. A few trees here and there rose above a low, marshy ground, which the colonists had already surveyed; and in violent contrast to the other desert shore, life was again manifested by the presence of myriads of water-fowl. That evening the *Bonadventure* anchored in a small bay to the north of the island, near the land, such was the depth of water there. The night passed quietly, for the breeze died away with the last light of day, and only rose again with the first streaks of dawn.

As it was easy to land, the usual hunters of the colony, that is to say, Herbert and Gideon Spilett, went for a ramble of two hours or so, and returned with several strings of wild duck and snipe. Top had done wonders, and not a bird had been lost, thanks to his zeal and cleverness.

At eight o'clock in the morning the *Bonadventure* set sail, and ran rapidly towards North Mandible Cape, for the wind was right astern and freshening rapidly.

"However," observed Pencroft, "I should not be surprised if a gale came up from the west. Yesterday the sun set in a very red-looking horizon, and now, this morning, those mares-tails don't forebode anything good."

These mares-tails are cirrus clouds, scattered in the zenith, their height from the sea being less than five thousand feet. They look like light pieces of cotton wool, and their presence usually announces some sudden change in the weather.

"Well," said Harding, "let us carry as much sail as possible, and run for shelter into Shark Gulf. I think that the *Bonadventure* will be safe there."

"Perfectly," replied Pencroft, "and besides, the north coast is merely sand, very uninteresting to look at."

"I shall not be sorry," resumed the engineer, "to pass not only to-night but to-morrow in that bay, which is worth being carefully explored."

"I think that we shall be obliged to do so, whether we like it or

153

not," answered Pencroft, "for the sky looks very threatening towards the west. Dirty weather is coming on!"

"At any rate we have a favourable wind for reaching Cape Mandible," observed the reporter.

"A very fine wind," replied the sailor; "but we must tack to enter the gulf, and I should like to see my way clear in these unknown quarters."

"Quarters which appear to be filled with rocks," added Herbert, "if we judge by what we saw on the south coast of Shark Gulf."

"Pencroft," said Cyrus Harding, "do as you think best, we will leave it to you."

"Don't make your mind uneasy, captain," replied the sailor, "I shall not expose myself needlessly! I would rather a knife were run into my ribs than a sharp rock into those of my *Bonadventure!*"

That which Pencroft called ribs was the part of his vessel under water, and he valued it more than his own skin.

"What o'clock is it?" asked Pencroft.

"Ten o'clock," replied Gideon Spilett.

"And what distance is it to the Cape, captain?"

"About fifteen miles," replied the engineer.

"That's a matter of two hours and a half," said the sailor, "and we shall be off the Cape between twelve and one o'clock. Unluckily, the tide will be turning at that moment, and will be ebbing out of the gulf. I am afraid that it will be very difficult to get in, having both wind and tide against us."

"And the more so that it is a full moon to-day," remarked Herbert, "and these April tides are very strong."

"Well, Pencroft," asked Cyrus Harding, "can you not anchor off the Cape?"

"Anchor near land, with bad weather coming on!" exclaimed the sailor. "What are you thinking of, captain? We should run aground to a certainty!"

"What will you do then?"

"I shall try to keep in the offing until the flood, that is to say, till about seven in the evening, and if there is still light enough I will try to enter the gulf; if not, we must stand off and on during the night, and we will enter to-morrow at sunrise."

"As I told you, Pencroft, we will leave it to you," answered Harding.

"Ah!" said Pencroft, "if there was only a light-house on the coast, it would be much more convenient for sailors."

"Yes," replied Herbert, "and this time we shall have no obliging engineer to light a fire to guide us into port!"

"Why, indeed, my dear Cyrus," said Spilett, "we have never thanked you for it, but frankly, without that fire we should never have been able to reach—"

"A fire?" asked Harding, much astonished at the reporter's words.

"We mean, captain," answered Pencroft, "that on board the *Bonadventure* we were very anxious during the few hours before our return, and we should have passed to windward of the island, if it had not been for the precaution you took of lighting a fire in the night of the 19th of October, on Prospect Heights."

"Yes, yes! That was a lucky idea of mine!" replied the engineer.

"And this time," continued the sailor, "unless the idea occurs to Ayrton, there will be no one to do us that little service!"

"No! no one!" answered Cyrus Harding.

A few minutes after, finding himself alone in the bows of the vessel with the reporter, the engineer bent down and whispered,—

"If there is one thing certain in this world, Spilett, it is that I never lighted any fire during the night of the 19th of October, neither on Prospect Heights nor on any other part of the island!"

CHAPTER XX

A Night at Sea—Shark Gulf—Confidences—Preparations for Winter—Forwardness of the bad Season—Severe Cold—Work in the Interior—In six Months—A photographic Negative—Unexpected Incident.

Things happened as Pencroft had predicted, he being seldom mistaken in his prognostications. The wind rose, and from a fresh breeze it soon increased to a regular gale; that is to say, it acquired a speed of from forty to forty-five miles an hour, before which a ship in the open sea would have run under close-reefed topsails. Now, as it was nearly six o'clock when the *Bonadventure* reached the gulf, and as at that moment the tide turned, it was impossible to enter. They were therefore compelled to stand off, for even if he had wished to do so, Pencroft could not have gained the mouth of the Mercy. Hoisting the jib to the mainmast by way of a storm-sail, he hove to, putting the head of the vessel towards the land.

Fortunately, although the wind was strong, the sea, being sheltered by the land, did not run very high. They had then little to fear from the waves, which always endanger small craft. The *Bonadventure* would doubtlessly not have capsized, for she was well ballasted; but enormous masses of water falling on the deck, might injure her, if her timbers could not sustain them. Pencroft, as a good sailor, was prepared for anything. Certainly, he had great confidence in his vessel, but nevertheless he awaited the return of day with some anxiety.

During the night, Cyrus Harding and Gideon Spilett had no opportunity for talking together, and yet the words pronounced in the reporter's ear by the engineer were well worth being discussed, together with the mysterious influence which appeared to reign over Lincoln Island. Gideon Spilett did not cease from pondering over this new and inexplicable incident,—the appearance of a fire on the coast of the island. The fire had actually been seen! His companions, Herbert and Pencroft, had seen it with him! The fire had served to signalise the position of the island during that dark night, and they had not doubted that it was lighted by the engineer's hand; and here was Cyrus Harding expressly declaring that he had never done anything of the sort! Spilett resolved to recur to this incident as soon as the *Bonadventure* returned, and to urge Cyrus Harding to acquaint their companions with these strange facts. Perhaps it would be decided to make in common a complete investigation of every part of Lincoln Island.

However that might be, on this evening no fire was lighted on these yet unknown shores, which formed the entrance to the gulf, and the little vessel stood off during the night.

When the first streaks of dawn appeared in the western horizon, the wind, which had slightly fallen, shifted two points, and enabled Pencroft to enter the narrow gulf with greater ease. Towards seven o'clock in the morning, the *Bonadventure*, weathering the North Mandible Cape, entered the strait and glided on to the waters, so strangely enclosed in the frame of lava.

"Well," said Pencroft, "this bay would make admirable roads, in which a whole fleet could lie at their ease!"

"What is especially curious," observed Harding, "is that the gulf has been formed by two rivers of lava, thrown out by the volcano, and accumulated by successive eruptions. The result is that the gulf is completely sheltered on all sides, and I believe that even in the stormiest weather, the sea here must be as calm as a lake."

"No doubt," returned the sailor, "since the wind has only that narrow entrance between the two capes to get in by; and besides, the north cape protects that of the south in a way which would make the entrance of gusts very difficult. I declare our *Bonadventure* could stay here from one end of the year to the other, without even dragging at her anchor!"

"It is rather large for her!" observed the reporter.

"Well! Mr. Spilett," replied the sailor, "I agree that it is too large for the *Bonadventure*; but if the fleets of the Union were in want of a harbour in the Pacific, I don't think they would ever find a better place than this!"

"We are in the shark's mouth," remarked Neb, alluding to the form of the gulf.

"Right into its mouth, my honest Neb!" replied Herbert; "but you are not afraid that it will shut upon us, are you?"

"No, Mr. Herbert," answered Neb; "and yet this gulf here doesn't please me much! It has a wicked look!"

"Hallo!" cried Pencroft, "here is Neb turning up his nose at my gulf, just as I was thinking of presenting it to America!"

"But, at any rate, is the water deep enough?" asked the engineer, "for a depth sufficient for the keel of the *Bonadventure*, would not be enough for those of our iron-clads."

"That is easily found out," replied Pencroft.

And the sailor sounded with a long cord, which served him as a lead-line, and to which was fastened a lump of iron. This cord measured nearly fifty fathoms, and its entire length was unrolled without finding any bottom.

"There," exclaimed Pencroft, "our iron-clads can come here after all! They would not run aground!"

"Indeed," said Gideon Spilett, "this gulf is a regular abyss; but, taking into consideration the volcanic origin of the island, it is not astonishing that the sea should offer similar depressions."

"One would say too," observed Herbert, "that these cliffs were perfectly perpendicular; and I believe that at their foot, even with a line five or six times longer, Pencroft would not find the bottom."

"That is all very well," then said the reporter; "but I must point out to Pencroft that his harbour is wanting in one very important respect!"

"And what is that, Mr. Spilett?"

"An opening, a cutting of some sort, to give access to the interior of the island. I do not see a spot on which we could land."

And, in fact, the steep lava cliffs did not afford a single place suitable for landing. They formed an insuperable barrier, recalling, but with more wildness, the fiords of Norway. The *Bonadventure*, coasting as close as possible along the cliffs, did not discover even a projection which would allow the passengers to leave the deck.

Pencroft consoled himself by saying that with the help of a mine they could soon open out the cliff when that was necessary, and then, as there was evidently nothing to be done in the gulf, he steered his vessel towards the strait and passed out at about two o'clock in the afternoon.

"Ah!" said Neb, uttering a sigh of satisfaction.

One might really say that the honest negro did not feel at his ease in those enormous jaws.

The distance from Mandible Cape to the mouth of the Mercy was not more than eight miles. The head of the *Bonadventure* was put towards Granite House, and a fair wind filling her sails, she ran rapidly along the coast.

To the enormous lava rocks succeeded soon those capricious sand dunes, among which the engineer had been so singularly recovered, and which sea-birds frequented in thousands.

About four o'clock, Pencroft, leaving the point of the islet on his left, entered the channel which separated it from the coast, and at five o'clock the anchor of the *Bonadventure* was buried in the sand at the mouth of the Mercy.

The colonists had been absent three days from their dwelling. Ayrton was waiting for them on the beach, and Jup came joyously to meet them, giving vent to deep grunts of satisfaction.

A complete exploration of the coast of the island had now been made, and no suspicious appearances had been observed. If any mysterious being resided on it, it could only be under cover of the impenetrable forest of the Serpentine Peninsula, to which the colonists had not yet directed their investigations.

Gideon Spilett discussed these things with the engineer, and it was agreed that they should direct the attention of their companions to the strange character of certain incidents which had occurred on the island, and of which the last was the most unaccountable.

However, Harding, returning to the fact of a fire having been kindled on the shore by an unknown hand, could not refrain from repeating for the twentieth time to the reporter—

"But are you quite sure of having seen it? Was it not a partial eruption of the volcano, or perhaps some meteor?"

"No, Cyrus," answered the reporter; "it was certainly a fire lighted by the hand of man. Besides, question Pencroft and Herbert. They saw it as I saw it myself, and they will confirm my words."

In consequence therefore, a few days after, on the 25th of April, in the evening, when the settlers were all collected on Prospect Heights, Cyrus Harding began by saying,—

"My friends, I think it my duty to call your attention to certain incidents which have occurred in the island, on the subject of which I shall be happy to have your advice. These incidents are, so to speak, supernatural—"

"Supernatural!" exclaimed the sailor, emitting a volume of smoke from his mouth. "Can it be possible that our island is supernatural?"

"No, Pencroft, but mysterious, most certainly," replied the engineer; "unless you can explain that which Spilett and I have until now failed to understand."

"Speak away, captain," answered the sailor.

"Well, have you understood," then said the engineer, "how was it that after falling into the sea, I was found a quarter of a mile into the interior of the island, and that, without my having any consciousness of my removal there?"

"Unless, being unconscious—" said Pencroft.

"That is not admissible," replied the engineer. "But to continue. Have you understood how Top was able to discover your retreat five miles from the cave in which I was lying?"

"The dog's instinct—" observed Herbert.

"Singular instinct!" returned the reporter; "since notwithstanding the storm of rain and wind which was raging

159

during that night, Top arrived at the Chimneys, dry and without a speck of mud!"

"Let us continue," resumed the engineer. "Have you understood how our dog was so strangely thrown up out of the waters of the lake, after his struggle with the dugong?"

"No! I confess, not at all," replied Pencroft; "and the wound which the dugong had in its side, a wound which seemed to have been made with a sharp instrument; that can't be understood either."

"Let us continue again," said Harding. "Have you understood, my friends, how that bullet got into the body of the young peccary; how that case happened to be so fortunately stranded, without there being any trace of a wreck; how that bottle containing the document presented itself so opportunely, during our first sea-excursion; how our canoe, having broken its moorings, floated down the current of the Mercy and rejoined us precisely at the very moment we needed it; how after the ape invasion the ladder was so obligingly thrown down from Granite House; and lastly, how the document, which Ayrton asserts was never written by him, fell into our hands?"

As Cyrus Harding thus enumerated, without forgetting one, the singular incidents which had occurred in the island, Herbert, Neb, and Pencraft stared at each other, not knowing what to reply, for this succession of incidents, grouped thus for the first time, could not but excite their surprise to the highest degree.

"'Pon my word," said Pencroft at last, "you are right, captain, and it is difficult to explain all these things!"

"Well, my friends," resumed the engineer, "a last fact has just been added to these, and it is no less incomprehensible than the others!"

"What is it, captain?" asked Herbert quickly.

"When you were returning from Tabor Island, Pencroft," continued the engineer, "you said that a fire appeared on Lincoln Island?"

"Certainly," answered the sailor.

"And you are quite certain of having seen this fire?"

"As sure as I see you now."

"You also, Herbert?"

"Why, captain," cried Herbert, "that fire was blazing like a star of the first magnitude!"

"But was it not a star?" urged the engineer.

"No," replied Pencroft, "for the sky was covered with thick clouds, and at any rate a star would not have been so low on the horizon. But Mr. Spilett saw it as well as we, and he will confirm our words."

"I will add," said the reporter, "that the fire was very bright, and that it shot up like a sheet of lightning."

"Yes, yes! exactly," added Herbert, "and it was certainly placed on the heights of Granite House."

"Well, my friends," replied Cyrus Harding, "during the night of the 19th of October, neither Neb nor I lighted any fire on the coast."

"You did not!" exclaimed Pencroft, in the height of his astonishment, not being able to finish his sentence.

"We did not leave Granite House," answered Cyrus Harding, "and if a fire appeared on the coast, it was lighted by another hand than ours!"

Pencraft, Herbert, and Neb were stupefied. No illusion could be possible, and a fire had actually met their eyes during the night of the 19th of October.

Yes! they were obliged to acknowledge it, a mystery existed! An inexplicable influence, evidently favourable to the colonists, but very irritating to their curiosity, was executed always in the nick of time on Lincoln Island. Could there be some being hidden in its profoundest recesses? It was necessary at any cost to ascertain this.

Harding also reminded his companions of the singular behaviour of Top and Jup when they prowled round the mouth of the well, which placed Granite House in communication with the sea, and he told them that he had explored the well, without discovering anything suspicious. The final resolve taken, in consequence of this conversation, by all the members of the colony, was that as soon as the fine season returned they would thoroughly search the whole of the island.

But from that day, Pencroft appeared to be anxious. He felt as if the island which he had made his own personal property belonged to him entirely no longer, and that he shared it with another master, to whom whether willing or not, he felt subject. Neb and he often talked of those unaccountable things, and both, their natures inclining them to the marvellous, were not far from believing that Lincoln Island was under the dominion of some supernatural power.

In the meanwhile, the bad weather came with the month of May, the November of the northern zones. It appeared that the winter would be severe and forward. The preparations for the winter season were therefore commenced without delay.

Nevertheless, the colonists were well prepared to meet the

winter, however hard it might be. They had plenty of felt clothing, and the musmons, very numerous by this time, had furnished an abundance of the wool necessary for the manufacture of this warm material.

It is unnecessary to say that Ayrton had been provided with this comfortable clothing. Cyrus Harding proposed that he should come to spend the bad season with them in Granite House, where he would be better lodged than at the corral, and Ayrton promised to do so, as soon as the last work at the corral was finished. He did this towards the middle of April. From that time Ayrton shared the common life, and made himself useful on all occasions; but still humble and sad, he never took part in the pleasures of his companions.

For the greater part of this, the third winter which the settlers passed in Lincoln Island, they were confined to Granite House. There were many violent storms and frightful tempests, which appeared to shake the rocks to their very foundations. Immense waves threatened to overwhelm the island, and certainly any vessel anchored near the shore would have been dashed to pieces. Twice, during one of these hurricanes, the Mercy swelled to such a degree as to give reason to fear that the bridges would be swept away, and it was necessary to strengthen those on the shore, which disappeared under the foaming waters, when the sea beat against the beach.

It may well be supposed that such storms, comparable to water-spouts in which were mingled rain and snow, would cause great havoc on the plateau of Prospect Heights. The mill and the poultry-yard particularly suffered. The colonists were often obliged to make immediate repairs, without which the safety of the birds would have been seriously threatened.

During the worst weather, several jaguars and troops of quadrumana ventured to the edge of the plateau, and it was always to be feared that the most active and audacious would, urged by hunger, manage to cross the stream, which besides, when frozen, offered them an easy passage. Plantations and domestic animals would then have been infallibly destroyed, without a constant watch, and it was often necessary to make use of the guns to keep those dangerous visitors at a respectful distance. Occupation was not wanting to the colonists, for without reckoning their out-door cares, they had always a thousand plans for the fitting up of Granite House.

They had also some fine sporting excursions, which were made during the frost in the vast Tadorn marsh. Gideon Spilett and

162

Herbert, aided by Jup and Top, did not miss a shot in the midst of the myriads of wild-duck, snipe, teal, and others. The access to these hunting-grounds was easy; besides, whether they reached them by the road to Port Balloon, after having passed the Mercy Bridge, or by turning the rocks from Flotsam Point, the hunters were never distant from Granite House more than two or three miles.

Thus passed the four winter months, which were really rigorous, that is to say, June, July, August, and September. But, in short, Granite House did not suffer much from the inclemency of the weather, and it was the same with the corral, which, less exposed than the plateau, and sheltered partly by Mount Franklin, only received the remains of the hurricanes, already broken by the forests and the high rocks of the shore. The damages there were consequently of small importance, and the activity and skill of Ayrton promptly repaired them, when some time in October he returned to pass a few days in the corral.

During this winter, no fresh inexplicable incident occurred. Nothing strange happened, although Pencroft and Neb were on the watch for the most insignificant facts to which they attached any mysterious cause. Top and Jup themselves no longer growled round the well or gave any signs of uneasiness. It appeared, therefore, as if the series of supernatural incidents was interrupted, although they often talked of them during the evenings in Granite House, and they remained thoroughly resolved that the island should be searched, even in those parts the most difficult to explore. But an event of the highest importance, and of which the consequence might be terrible, momentarily diverted from their projects Cyrus Harding and his companions.

It was the month of October. The fine season was swiftly returning. Nature was reviving; and among the evergreen foliage of the coniferæ which formed the border of the wood, already appeared the young leaves of the banksias, deodars, and other trees.

It may be remembered that Gideon Spilett and Herbert had, at different times, taken photographic views of Lincoln Island.

Now, on the 17th of this month of October, towards three o'clock in the afternoon, Herbert, enticed by the charms of the sky, thought of reproducing Union Bay, which was opposite to Prospect Heights, from Cape Mandible to Claw Cape.

The horizon was beautifully clear, and the sea, undulating under a soft breeze, was as calm as the waters of a lake, sparkling here and there under the sun's rays.

The apparatus had been placed at one of the windows of the dining-room at Granite House, and consequently overlooked the shore and the bay. Herbert proceeded as he was accustomed to do, and the negative obtained, he went away to fix it by means of the chemicals deposited in a dark nook of Granite House.

Returning to the bright light, and examining it well, Herbert perceived on his negative an almost imperceptible little spot on the sea horizon. He endeavoured to make it disappear by reiterated washing, but could not accomplish it.

"It is a flaw in the glass," he thought.

And then he had the curiosity to examine this flaw with a strong magnifier which he unscrewed from one of the telescopes.

But he had scarcely looked at it, when he uttered a cry, and the glass almost fell from his hands.

Immediately running to the room in which Cyrus Harding then was, he extended the negative and magnifier towards the engineer, pointing out the little spot.

Harding examined it; then seizing his telescope he rushed to the window.

The telescope, after having slowly swept the horizon, at last stopped on the looked-for spot, and Cyrus Harding lowering it, pronounced one word only,—

"A vessel!"

And in fact a vessel was in sight, off Lincoln Island!